OSWAIN AND THE BATTLE FOR ALAMORE

For Ben

Oswain
and the
Battle for Alamore

JOHN HOUGHTON

KINGSWAY PUBLICATIONS
EASTBOURNE

First published 1984 as *Hagbane's Doom*
This substantially revised edition 2001

ISBN 0 85476 962 5

Published by
KINGSWAY PUBLICATIONS
Lottbridge Drove, Eastbourne, BN23 6NT, England.
Email: books@kingsway.co.uk

Designed and produced for the publishers by
Bookprint Creative Services, P.O. Box 827, BN21 3YJ, England.
Printed in Great Britain.

Contents

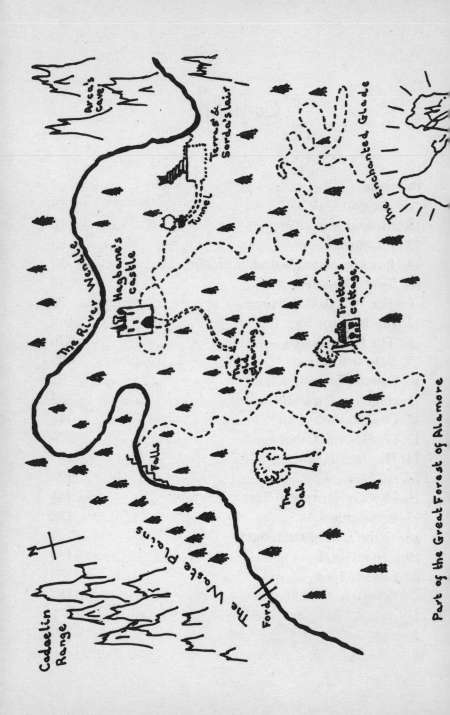

Part of the Great Forest of Alamore

Prologue

Our story begins with a young prince who had a dream. It took place one night in the realm that some call The Land Beyond the Far Places but which, like many such lands, is maybe closer than you think – the amazing world of Caris Meriac. The prince's name was Oswain and this was his dream.

A single candle burned in the empty night. The flame beckoned Oswain and he drifted towards its hypnotic glow until its light filled the dark dream space in which he floated. Three faces swam into the light – a freckle-faced boy, a girl with deep, dark eyes, and a smiling young lad, each so alive, so real that he wanted to speak to them; but they simply faded away into the flame. Oswain wondered who they could be.

A gust of wind blew upon the flame so that it flickered in a wild confusion of light. Another image began to form and his heart beat faster, for never before had he seen such an evil-looking face. For a brief moment it hovered before him, the glaring, red-rimmed eyes so hateful that he would have turned and fled if he could. But our dreams do not let us run away, and so he watched in horror until at last the face dissolved to ashes, and only the flame burned on.

With a quiet hiss, the tongue of fire parted down the middle to reveal the deep space that lay beyond the stars. It seemed a lonely place. Then Oswain spied a single dot of light in the far distance. The light grew in size, rushing towards him at such a speed that almost at once it filled the screen of his mind with its dazzling brightness. A splendid jewel hung before his eyes.

'The Merestone,' whispered Oswain.

He awoke with a start to find himself lying on the floor of his bedchamber. Trembling slightly, he rose and crossed to the window. All was quiet as he gazed out across the sleeping city over which his father, King Argil, ruled. Then, almost without his being aware of it, he looked up into the night sky where, hanging like a pearl in the velvet blackness, one star gleamed more brightly than the rest. He glanced at the ring on his second finger. The silver sliver of stone it contained glinted in response.

'My destiny calls me. Elmesh has spoken.' He uttered the words quietly but firmly to himself and then turned to prepare for the journey that lay ahead.

* * *

High in that same night sky, though many miles distant, in the stark emptiness of the snow-covered mountains a mighty white eagle felt a light tug in the wind. It was nothing more, but Arca, whose senses were tuned to the finest degree, knew that he had received a command. His time had also come, and from that moment he flew steadily south.

The adventure was about to begin.

1
The Old Oak

'Hoi! Mind my head, Peter. Ouch!'

'I can't help it, this old ladder's falling to pieces. I'm doing my best.'

'Oh, stop moaning you two and get on with it,' said Andrew from lower down the ladder. 'Anyway, I don't know what you're complaining about, Sarah, 'cos if it breaks, I get you both on top of me!'

'Well, it'll just give us a soft landing, then,' called Peter. 'Perhaps we should try it and see!'

Andrew laughed. 'Just you dare!'

The three Brown children were climbing a massive oak tree at the far end of Uncle Joe's orchard. It was the Spring Bank Holiday and they had come down to stay for a week at his cottage just outside the historic and beautiful village of Abbotsbury in Dorset.

Uncle Joe lived alone and was rather old fashioned; he didn't have a computer or any games other than Happy Families, draughts and Scrabble, and even the television didn't work properly. It looked like being one of those holidays where you just wish you were back home. To make matters worse they hadn't even been able to bring their mountain bikes with them. The gearbox had failed on their father's car just a day before their holidays and the car loaned to him by the garage was simply too small to carry the family and three bikes as well.

Peter was the most upset; he had just had a new bike for his birthday and was longing to try it out somewhere other than the streets around home. Forced instead to traipse round the Swannery and the subtropical gardens with his parents and brother and sister for the whole morning, he had sulked all the way. By lunch time, Sarah and Andrew were as bad, and after eating back at Uncle Joe's, their father told them to go off and play in the garden to give the grown-ups a bit of peace and quiet.

Uncle Joe owned quite a lot of land including a large garden, a vegetable plot and an old orchard. The orchard was farthest from the cottage and the children had wandered among the spreading apple and pear trees until they reached the edge of a piece of woodland. It was there that they spotted the old oak.

They eyed the great tree with its massive trunk and its branches rustling with bright green new leaves.

'We've got to climb it,' said Peter, who was feeling a bit better.

'Why?' asked Sarah.

'I dunno. It's there, that's all,' he answered. 'Come on. It'll be fun.'

A brief search back in the orchard produced a rather ancient fruit-picking ladder that would get them to the lowest boughs and, after a brief debate as to who should go first (which ended as it nearly always did), they began to climb in age order.

Peter was twelve. He wore a Manchester United sweatshirt with his jeans, and had an untidy mop of brown hair. He liked nothing better than to be riding his bike or kicking a football. In fact, he had recently suggested to his teacher, Mr Pyle, the idea of cycle football using bikes with engines rather than pedals so that the players' legs were free to kick the ball. Mr Pyle had muttered something about buckled wheels and broken legs and him taking early retirement – and no, it was unlikely to become a new Olympic sport!

Peter's younger sister, Sarah, was a thoughtful ten-year-old who enjoyed watching waves beat on the seashore, and the way the rain fell on her eyelashes. Everyone said she was a day dreamer, but she preferred to call it imagination, and said it stopped her getting bored in lessons. Her best teachers had the sense to tell her to write down her day dreams. Today she was wearing her favourite black leggings and a sea-green fleece jacket over a World Wildlife Fund T-shirt. She had put her blonde hair into a ponytail with a poppy-red scrunchie.

Nine-year-old Andrew made up the terrible trio, as their father called them. He was wearing a denim jacket over a green check shirt and jeans, and as usual, a cheeky grin. Andrew was always making up daft jokes. His latest was, 'What do you call someone who kills bikes? A cycle path!'

All three children, at their mother's insistence, had on their oldest trainers.

You will have realised perhaps that these were the three faces that Oswain had seen in his dream.

'Wow, there's a smashing fork in the tree up here. Come on, you two. We can build a tree house, and then pretend we're being attacked by natives and wild animals and have to live off emergency rations.' Peter began to clamber among the branches.

'And then Mum will call us in for tea,' puffed Sarah as

she scrambled up to join him.

'Wow, what a view,' gasped Andrew as he looked around. 'You can see right over the orchard from here. It's fantastic! We must be miles up. What do you think, Sarah, eh?'

Before his sister could answer, Peter called them over to the other side of the great fork in the tree.

'Hey, you two, come and have a look at this. I've found this massive great hole.'

Andrew and Sarah joined him.

'It's big enough to get into, if you crouch,' said Sarah. 'Do you think we should try?'

'There's probably a gorilla or a snake hiding in there. Creep inside and it'll grab you by the throat . . .' Andrew tried to imitate what it was like to be strangled by a gorilla four metres up in a tree. The others looked at him and shook their heads sadly.

Peter was peering into the hole. 'It's very dark. Can't see much. Maybe it's an owl's nest, though I don't know.' His eyes began to adjust to the gloom. 'It seems to go in quite a way and then it drops down. Perhaps the tree is hollow. Weird. I'm going to have a look.'

So saying, he crept inside – and discovered something he really never expected to find.

'Hey, this is odd, there are steps leading down into the tree,' he exclaimed. 'Come and look.'

The three of them crowded in as best they could and stared in amazement. There, sure enough, was a flight of wooden stairs descending steeply into the tree trunk.

'Very clever gorilla, that's all I can say,' said Peter.

'How did they get there?'

'Where do they go?'

'We've got to explore it. This is fantastic!'

'Yes, let's see how far down they go,' Peter suggested.

'I don't know. I'm not sure I want to. Don't you think we should tell Mum first and ...' But Sarah never finished her sentence. One glance at her brothers' faces was enough. 'Oh, all right, I'm coming,' she said.

Whatever it was that possessed Peter, Sarah and Andrew to descend into the warm brownness of the great tree none of them could afterwards explain. It was almost as though it was meant to happen. Yet if Peter, or his brother and sister, had any doubts they were dispelled as each one passed the seventh step down. It wasn't much – just the briefest shimmer of silver blue light that made each one of them shiver and left them tingly and goose bumpy all over – but they knew that they had passed through some kind of invisible gate and that they must go ever deeper into the darkness, and to whatever awaited them.

'It must go right to the bottom of the tree at this rate,' muttered Peter.

'More like the bottom of the world,' Sarah replied. She was wondering if they would ever get out again.

'Hey, I can see daylight. It must come out at ground level.'

'That's odd though, 'cos I've counted fifty steps so far,' Andrew exclaimed.

'Hmm, still here we are back in the gar. . .' Peter stared and shivered. Suddenly, he felt queasy.

'What is it, Pete? What's the matter? Oh! Oh, no!'

'It's not our garden!'

The children stared blankly at the scene that confronted them. Instead of a pleasant spring orchard they were surrounded by a vast forest of ancient grey trees whose winter bare branches reached up into a cold pale mist. Many other branches lay broken on the ground. The sour smell of decay hung in the dank air and all was silent. Lifeless, as still as death.

'Wh-where are we?' stuttered Sarah. 'It's like some kind of petrified forest. I don't like it at all. Can we go back? I said we shouldn't have come.'

'Oh, shush a moment, will you?' said Peter, trying to gather his wits. 'Let me think. Something odd has happened to us and I don't know what it is, but let's not go back – at least, not yet.'

The three children stood in silence while they pondered their plight.

'The seventh step down, it was,' Andrew said, breaking the silence. 'That's when I felt all kind of funny inside. You know what I think's happened? I reckon it's like in science fiction when you go into a para . . . what-do-you-call-it?'

'Parallel universe,' prompted Peter.

'That's it. One of those. Anyway,' he continued, 'if that's what's happened to us then we ought to find out what it's all about. I think we should take a look round. But watch out for aliens or robots with death rays.'

Peter said thoughtfully, 'Maybe it's just that we've gone back in time – or maybe forwards. We could still be in the same place.'

By now Sarah had stopped shaking and was feeling better. 'I don't know which it is, but I had the feeling too, and it wasn't a bad one, so I think it's all right. It's silly to be afraid, I suppose.' She looked at Peter. 'I'm OK. Lead on, then. But let's be careful, just in case.'

They wrapped the scrunchie from Sarah's pony-tail over a small branch on the oak to help them find it again. Andrew wished he had a laser gun but he had to make do with a broken branch and pretend.

'There's hardly a sign of life anywhere,' said Peter. 'The forest is almost dead. Just a bit of moss and a few bushes growing here and there. I wonder what happened to it?'

'Mmm, it's not dead but, well, as though someone has taken all the life out of it.'

'Well it must be dead then,' laughed Andrew.

'No, that's not what I mean. What I'm trying to say is…'

Before Sarah could explain there was a sudden rustling and crashing from the dead undergrowth nearby and, in a twinkling of an eye, they were surrounded, not by aliens or robots, but by a gang of fierce-looking animals all armed with spears and clubs.

'One move and you die! Stay right where you are.' The speaker was an important-looking stoat.

The children could not have moved even if they had tried. It's bad enough to find yourself where you did not, even in your wildest dreams, expect to be. But to be confronted by animals the same size as you, that speak – well, that is a bit too much. Robots might have made more sense.

The ring of animals closed in – rabbits, foxes, weasels, moles, squirrels. Their fierce eyes and bared teeth made it quite clear that they were far from friendly. And the prods and pricks that the children received were real enough to prove that this was no dream.

'Tie them up and take them away,' the stoat commanded.

At once, the animals swarmed over the children, pushing them to the ground. Sarah started to scream but a gag was promptly pushed into her mouth. Rough ropes bound their hands behind their backs and, in spite of their frantic struggles, it seemed only a matter of seconds before they were quite helpless. They were dragged to their feet and, encouraged by the spears, were shoved along a narrow twisting pathway that led off into the undergrowth.

As they stumbled along, Peter began to pull himself together. Wherever they were, and whether they had been brought here by science or by magic, one thing was clear – they had fallen into the hands of hostile creatures and they had to escape as soon as they could. That was obviously not possible at the moment, so he tried instead to keep track of the twists and turns in the hope that they might find their way back to the old oak when they did escape.

It proved an impossible task, however, since many paths criss-crossed their route and often they would be forced to the left or to the right down yet another winding track. Soon he was totally confused.

He noticed that the pace was hotting up and many of the animals were casting nervous glances over their shoulders as though expecting to be chased. Perhaps there was someone who would come to their rescue, Peter thought, and this cheered him up a little.

The company was almost running by the time they reached the end of the trail and they came at last to a panting halt in a small clearing. The children fought to get their breath through the smelly gags. If only they could speak.

The stoat, who was obviously in command, nodded to their closest captors and the three children were pushed forwards in the direction of a tall, imposing elm tree. At first, they couldn't see why. Then they noticed a dark hole near the roots. Sarah wondered if this led upstairs to home or downstairs to somewhere else. Andrew thought it might be a prison. Prods from behind soon had all three crowded reluctantly in the entrance and staring into the gloom.

It was Peter who saw them first. A pair of slant yellow eyes glowed out of the darkness and began to move towards them! Panic welled up inside them, and the children's minds filled with all kinds of nameless dreads about child-eating monsters. Wildly, they turned to run but were met squarely by a mass of sharp-pointed spears that would allow them no escape.

Slowly but surely the helpless children were driven backwards into the black hole, there to meet whatever unknown horror awaited them in its depths.

2

Mr and Mrs Trotter

'What do you want done with 'em, Aldred, sir?'

The eyes spoke and materialised into the form of a smart-looking fox.

'Are they spies? More of *her* work, eh!'

'That's right, Foxy,' the stoat replied. 'Caught them up by the old oak. Strange creatures, aren't they? Not like her usual work and not very strong either. We overpowered them with hardly a struggle.'

'What weapons did they have, sir?'

'That's the odd thing, they've got none. Unless it's some secret magic we don't know about. That's why I want Trotter to see them.'

'Very good, sir. I'll fetch him.'

The children were pushed through a door at the end of a short dark tunnel and found themselves standing in a small bare room that was lit from a window high up on one pale yellow wall. Relief flooded through them as they realised that Foxy was only a guard and not some terrible monster about to devour them. The room appeared to be quite civilised and they hoped that this Trotter, whoever he was, would allow them to explain who they were.

They had not long to wait. Another door opened and in walked an ancient badger.

Aldred stepped forward smartly and saluted. All the

other animals had remained outside, with the exception of a hedgehog who continued to menace them with his fearsome bristles.

'Strange spies, Trotter, sir. We caught them by the old oak. Truth is, sir, I don't know quite what to make of them, so I brought them to you as soon as possible. What do you think she's up to this time?'

The badger stepped forward and peered at the children through wire-rimmed spectacles. Sarah thought he had kind eyes. For about a minute, he looked them over, not saying a word. Then he spoke in a low voice. 'Loose their bonds and remove those gags.'

This task was quickly performed and with great sighs of relief the children rubbed their sore wrists and stretched their aching muscles. Peter was just about to blurt out a mixture of questions and explanations when the badger held up a paw. Then, to the amazement of everyone in the room, he slowly went down on one knee before them.

'Children of Time Beyond Time, for that is who you are, is it not?' he asked gravely. 'My name is Trotter and I bid you welcome to the Great Forest of Alamore in the world we know as Caris Meriac. You have come as it is written. May Elmesh be praised! I ask you to forgive us for the rude welcome that we gave you, but these are perilous days, and we did not know the hour of your coming. Nor would it have been wise for us to know, lest our enemy were to discover it. My guards were only doing their duty.'

Before anybody else could speak, Aldred blurted out, 'But are you sure, sir? Are you saying these are on our side? That Elmesh has sent them?'

The badger's eyes twinkled. 'Of course. Did I not tell you that I had received indications of their coming and of what to look for?' He rose and turned to Peter. 'It is true that you are the Children of Time Beyond Time?'

Peter found himself stammering. 'W-w-well, y-yes, I suppose so. I-I don't really know. We aren't usually called that – we're just people, kids, that's all. Listen, what *is* all this? Where are we? How is it you can speak? I don't understand what's happened to us. Is it all some kind of a dream?'

Trotter rumbled a deep laugh in his throat. 'Too many questions at once. And I thought you were coming with answers! Never mind, never mind. Elmesh has strange ways. I will answer your questions as best I can. But first, I think, a cup of tea would be in order. You must come and meet Mrs Trotter. She will be most interested to see you.'

There was a kindly authority in the badger's voice and Sarah warmed to him at once. 'A cup of tea would be fantastic,' she said, 'and we'd love to meet Mrs Trotter.'

With great politeness the badger ushered them through the door by which he had entered. If the world had seemed strange up until now, for a moment at least it became almost normal. They found themselves standing in a delightful cottage room complete with gleaming brasses and glowing copper kettles, wooden beams and soft armchairs. A small log fire burned in the smoke-blackened fireplace and flowery curtains decorated the leaded windows. They had entered by a kind of back door into the badger's home.

'What a pretty house!' exclaimed Sarah. 'It's beautiful!'

'I'm glad you like it, my dear.' Mrs Trotter bustled in, wearing a frilly apron. 'You're very welcome to our house. That is, if you're not friends of *hers*.'

'My dear, may I introduce you to the Children of Time Beyond Time – um, people. They have come as I said.'

'Oh well, pleased to meet you, I'm sure, but is that the only name you have?' she enquired. 'It's quite a mouthful, my dears.'

The children took to her at once and Andrew replied cheerily, 'It's nice to meet you too Mrs T. Can I call you Mrs T – because you're going to make the tea, and it's the first letter of Trotter? I'm Andrew ... Andrew Brown, and she's Sarah, and that's Peter.'

Peter and Sarah looked daggers at their younger brother because of his cheek, but Mrs Trotter laughed. 'Why, that's better. Of course you can. You are so serious sometimes, dear,' she scolded her husband. 'Well, I expect you would like that nice cup of tea,' she said to the children. 'Make yourselves at home. Sit down, my dears.'

She bustled back to the kitchen as they flopped into the armchairs. 'It's good to meet your wife, Mr Trotter,' said Peter, smiling, 'but please answer some of our questions.'

'Yes, of course,' replied the badger, settling himself into an old sofa by the fireside. 'So, you do not know where you are, or why you are here? That is strange, but perhaps hardly surprising as the utmost secrecy will have been kept by Elmesh. But that is *very* secret: not even to tell the deliverers who they are!' He smiled to himself.

'Um, excuse me, but who is El ... Elmesh?' interrupted Sarah.

'Elmesh, who is Elmesh?' exclaimed Trotter, sitting up with a blink of surprise that made his spectacles jump. 'You don't know? Elmesh just *is*. Without Elmesh there would be nothing, nothing at all. No sun, no stars, no Caris Meriac, not even the Great Forest of Alamore.' The badger shook his head in amazement. 'Nobody has told you that? Goodness gracious me! Yet it is surely obvious that Elmesh has sent you!'

'But all we did was climb a tree and go down some steps inside,' said Andrew. 'I just don't get it. And what did you say this place was?'

'Ah, that tree! There is something special about that oak, you see. It is a sort of doorway, though only at certain times, I believe.' He nodded sagely and looked at the three children in turn. 'You have entered the world of Caris Meriac, what the wise also call The Land Beyond The Far Places.'

'You mean, we're in some kind of fifth dimension,' said Andrew.

'Fifth dimension, eh?' Trotter answered with a smile. 'Well, maybe, but I think you will find there is a lot more to it than that.'

'We're not dead then . . . or dreaming?' Sarah queried. She had begun to wonder.

'My goodness me, no. Why should you ever think that?' Trotter chuckled. 'No, you'll probably feel more awake than ever once you grow used to things!'

Sarah smiled.

'You said we were to be deliverers,' said Peter. 'What did you mean?'

Trotter's answer was delayed by the entry of Mrs Trotter laden with tea and cakes. For a few minutes nobody said a word as they devoured the delicious goodies set before them. Then Trotter said he would try to begin at the beginning.

'Years ago, before our present troubles began, the Great Forest of Alamore was beautiful and fair to look upon. Birds sang in every tree and scented shrubs bloomed everywhere. The forest-folk roamed free and food was plentiful.' Trotter's eyes gazed into the distance. 'I remember those days when I was young,' he said. 'What great times we had. Not a care in the world. We all knew Elmesh looked after things and we used to visit the Enchanted Glade sometimes to look at the Merestone. The elders taught us that this wonderful jewel was the secret of the forest's beauty and certainly to be near it was a most wonderful experience. Why, if you hurt yourself, just to go there made you better. And those who desired wisdom spent long hours gazing at it and learning the ways of Elmesh.'

'Did you do that?' asked Sarah eagerly.

'Yes, I did, but as I say it seems a long time ago now, for, alas, all that has changed. A great tragedy fell upon us. *She* came one fateful day and stole the Merestone.' His face filled with sorrow as he spoke. 'Then she returned to enslave the Great Forest. Our happy days came to an end. The forest began to wither and die all around us; flowers ceased blooming and almost all the birds fled. Food has become scarce and the forest-folk live in fear of their lives. That is why we have to defend ourselves,' he explained.

'But who is *she*?' queried Peter.

'Hagbane!' Aldred, who had been listening, spat the word out. 'Hagbane the Shadow-witch. She stole the Merestone and brought this evil upon us. She controls us all from her castle and nobody can touch her while she holds it. We are almost helpless.' His shoulders sagged

and the children could sense the sorrow of a brave
soldier fighting on but knowing he had lost the battle.

'Well, I'm not afraid of any silly Shadow-witch,
whatever she is. We'll just go and kick her door in and
get your Merestone back!' declared Andrew stoutly.

'Oh, shush, Andrew!' exclaimed Sarah. 'Listen.'

'Alas, I do not think it will be quite that simple,' Trotter
continued. 'Yes, I do believe you will help deliver us
from Hagbane's power, for it is written that it should be
so, but you will find that she is no light foe to tackle.
Many of our folk have tried and as a result now languish
in her dungeons, or worse.'

'Where do we fit into all this?' enquired Peter. 'Because
we seem to be the most unlikely Shadow-witch fighters I
can think of, whatever my little brother says.'

Andrew glowered at him but said nothing.

In answer to the question the badger ushered them
into another room filled with dusty brown books and
parchments.

'I have studied the ways of Elmesh all my life. Many
hours I have sat in the Enchanted Glade and gazed into
the pool. Often I have looked upon the light of the star,
Elrilion, Elmesh's star, as it reflected in the water. To
myself alone were entrusted the ancient scrolls of the
Great Forest of Alamore so that I am the recognised lore-
master among the forest-folk.' He paused. 'Five nights
ago I had a vision in my sleep in which I saw your faces
by the light of Elrilion. I knew the time was at hand and
I read the prophecy again.'

'Can we see what it says?' chorused the children.

'It is written in an ancient script but I will translate it
roughly for you.' He took up an old yellowed parchment

covered in strange symbols and began to read:

> They will come from time beyond time,
> A sign the Merestone will mend;
> To judge the Shadow-witch's crime,
> Children the oak steps descend.
>
> A true king will come to his throne,
> Through a path of fire and pain;
> But he shall not struggle alone;
> Together his crown we'll gain.
>
> Rise up and take heart for the fight,
> We must set the forest free;
> Dispelling the dark with the light;
> Giving life to fur and tree!

'I confess I do not understand more than a part of this, but it is obvious that you have come, and we must start from there.'

'But are you sure it's really us it's talking about?' Peter asked. 'Could you be mistaken? After all, we're only ordinary children. We've no magic powers or weapons. What can we do against this horrible Shadow-witch creature?'

Trotter looked Peter straight in the eye. 'Elmesh does not deceive. It *is* you and inside I believe you know that it is so.' He spoke with such gravity that Peter felt he could only nod in agreement. Sarah and Andrew found their heads nodding also.

'Nor will you be quite weaponless, for I have this to give you.' As he spoke, he unlocked a small chest and from it drew what looked like a large powder compact covered in green tarnish. He handled the object with great reverence. 'This is Gilmere, mighty mirror of the Merestone. My father, Rufus the Strong, entrusted it to me. I have kept it for this day.'

He handed the object to Peter who took it gingerly. 'What do we do with it and how will it help us?' he enquired.

'If you press the clasp it will spring open and let forth its secret. But do point it away from us all, and use it wisely.'

Peter held the mirror in the palm of his hand and did as he was instructed. The lid flipped open, releasing a blaze of dazzling light that filled the room with a terrible but wonderful radiance. Andrew found himself riding a wild roller-coaster of sparkling golden fire on tracks of shimmering silver laser beams, while Sarah saw fiery angels spinning flying webs of rainbow coloured jewels all around her. So dizzying was the sight that it was something of a relief when Peter snapped the lid shut.

'Wow, impressive! What is it?' he gasped.

'Nobody rightly knows, except that it is a mirror formed by the hand of Elmesh in Elmere. That is the name we give to the Enchanted Glade and more particularly to the pool itself. Maybe the mirror is a shard of the Merestone or of something else. I do not know. But it has captured some of the light of the Merestone and though it has not its power it will, nonetheless, serve those who use it rightly in the battle against evil.'

'Why didn't Hagbane steal this too?' asked Andrew.

'Because she doesn't know of its existence, or at least, did not. For she has discovered many secrets from her captives since she first arrived. When Hagbane came she had eyes only for the jewel. Gilmere was kept hidden and, I believe, was watched over by Elmesh. My father gave it to me on his deathbed. I give it now to you to use with a true heart.'

The children gazed in awe at the innocent object in Peter's hand.

'Thank you for trusting us, Mr Trotter,' whispered Sarah. 'We'll do our best to look after it, and use it wisely.' She looked at her brothers, but before they could agree, a bloodcurdling shriek rent the air and struck a chill to the marrow of their bones. The next instant, the door crashed open and in stumbled Foxy.

'It's Hagbane!' he gasped. 'She's just down the path and she's caught Sam Squirrel. I think she's killing him!'

3

Captured!

The shock of hearing such a scream followed by Foxy's dramatic entry left everyone stunned for a few moments. It was Peter who snapped out of it first.

'Come on, everybody,' he cried. 'Let's try and stop her.'

Sarah tried to shout 'wait', but before she or anyone else could protest he was out of the door urging Foxy to show the way, rapidly followed by Aldred the stoat. Andrew and Sarah glanced at each other then ran after their brother. Trotter followed more slowly, looking extremely worried.

The three children and Foxy rushed down the forest path. The sounds of a struggle grew louder and, as they rounded a bend, they came upon the cause of the commotion. Hanging in mid-air and struggling for all he was worth in what seemed to be an invisible grip was the hapless Sam Squirrel. The children stared, horrified by the sight of his bulging eyes and the choking sounds that came from his mouth.

Sarah tore her eyes away and then looked again. A vague shape began to materialise; there, in the middle of the path, stood a shadowy twisted figure whose bony fingers clutched the squirrel about his throat. Sarah stared with horror as the vile creature took shape before her: the long black cloak that seemed like the darkness itself, the greasy grey hair tumbling wildly about her shoulders, the cruel eyes and long, distorted nose covered in warts, and the mouth twisted in a snarl of hatred. A stench of evil hung in the air around her, and it felt icy cold. Worst of all, Sarah seemed able almost to see through her as though the creature wasn't quite solid.

They had come face to face with the Shadow-witch.

She glanced at them with hard eyes glinting red and dropped the squirrel to the ground where he lay, a limp bundle of fur, at her feet. With a snarl of rage she drew a long black rod from the folds of her cloak. There was a blinding flash and a cloud of smoke, and when it cleared children and animals alike found themselves rooted to the spot. Full of menace, the Shadow-witch advanced and they prepared themselves as best they could for whatever awful fate she had in store for them.

All except Peter, that is.

For Peter Brown was seeing differently from the rest of the company. A strange spell had fallen upon him and before his eyes stood not an ugly crone but the most beautiful woman he had ever seen. She had blonde hair that cascaded over a dress of finest silver lace, almond eyes and full ruby lips. With a subtle smile she beckoned to Peter and showed him the finest mountain bike he had ever set eyes upon, brand new and gleaming with chrome and bright red and silver paint. Totally entranced by the sight, Peter walked slowly towards her.

The others watched, horrified and helpless, as the hypnotised Peter was drawn towards the horrible darkness of Hagbane. Sarah tried to cry out, but could not speak, such was the power of the spell that the Shadow-witch had cast over them.

Peter, his eyes riveted on the bike, reached Hagbane's

side. It had everything: alloy frame, triple chainset, front and rear suspension, 21-speed gripshift, V-type brakes – it was just all there. He reached eagerly for the handlebars and, as he did so, his fingers let slip the precious mirror, Gilmere. The Shadow-witch glanced down and sneered. Then, with a cackling laugh, she ground the object beneath the heel of her shoe. In spite of her shadowyness her foot proved solid enough and the onlookers heard the splintering of a thousand shards of glass. Poor Trotter felt his heart break at the sound. The fight was over before it had even started.

Taking the mesmerised Peter's hand in her own, Hagbane led him away into the depths of the Great Forest and towards her own castle. He held his other hand at an angle as though he were wheeling a bike, though, as the others could see, no such machine existed outside of his own deceived imagination.

For what seemed like an age none of the rest could move and only when Hagbane was well out of sight did the spell begin to wear off. Slowly, limbs regained their movement and tongues could again speak.

Trotter groaned. 'Oh dear, dear me. How dreadful this is! If only he had used Gilmere wisely instead of rushing out like that. And now all is lost and ruined.' He sat down on the ground, a heap of despair, his hopes as shattered as the remains of the mirror that lay at his feet.

The others stood around awkwardly and although Andrew felt Trotter was being unfair to Peter, he said nothing. At last Aldred broke the silence with a polite cough.

'Shall I round up a party to go after them, sir?'

The stoat's tone of voice said it all – it was hopeless.

Trotter shook his grey head slowly.

'No, that will not do. You will never catch her now and it would harm the boy in any case. No, let me think for a moment.'

Sarah, though she felt sick with worry for her elder brother, put her arm gently around the old badger.

'Come on, Mr Trotter. Don't give up. I'm sure there's an answer. If what you say is true and the one you call Elmesh has sent us, then somehow this is all *meant*. It's got to be all right. It must be,' she added fiercely. 'We *must* get Peter back. Although goodness knows how.'

Trotter looked up into her face and smiled. He patted her hand. 'Yes, of course we must and we will if it's at all possible. Silly me. I just felt so taken aback by the turn of events. So excited to see you and then crushed by . . . by this. I'm getting old, my dear, and not used to such suddenness. You do understand, don't you?'

Sarah smiled and kissed the old badger and felt she loved him.

'Well,' he said, getting up. 'I know Hagbane well enough; she isn't going to kill Peter, otherwise she would have done so at once. My guess is that she will use him as a hostage in some way, and that gives us a little time to plan.'

He gazed at the smashed mirror and made a decision. 'First of all, we must gather up every fragment of the mirror, for tonight we shall need it all.'

While he performed this task, placing each piece with care into a spotted handkerchief, the others tended to poor Sam Squirrel. Fortunately, they had been in time and he seemed set to make a quick recovery.

'Sh . . . she just appeared from nowhere and grabbed

me,' he gasped. 'I don't know why. I wasn't doing anything.'

Grim-faced, Aldred looked up at Sarah and Andrew. 'It appears to have been a deliberate decoy to get us here. I think she knew of your coming.' His eyes narrowed suspiciously and the children knew at once that the stoat did not trust them. That, and the possibility that Hagbane could read the signs too – that she could know – made them feel very uncomfortable. Sarah shivered and realised that it was growing dark.

'Can we go back to your house, please?' she asked quietly.

Trotter glanced at the dying sun and the lengthening shadows of the gaunt trees, and nodded. He seemed to understand how the children felt.

Night had fallen by the time they reached the cottage door and the first stars were appearing. Trotter stopped and pointed with his paw to where there was a gap between the treetops. A bright star that glittered like a globule of molten silver lay just above the horizon. The sight of it brought an unexpected trickle of hope into their hearts.

'Elrilion has risen,' whispered Trotter. 'All will be well. You'll see.'

*   *   *

High in an empty mountain pass, Prince Oswain saw that same star and was glad. For several days he had trudged through the foothills of the Cadaelin range of mountains until he had begun to climb a high pass known as the Dragon's Claw. Once he made it through to the other side he knew he would be in sight of the Great Forest of Alamore. It was then that the blizzard had struck. Visibility was reduced to zero as the snow beat against his face and the line between sky and mountain disappeared in a complete whiteout. Fierce winds seemed intent on tearing him from his path and dashing him on the rocks far below. Soon he was struggling knee deep in snow.

Night fell, but still he battled on. His destiny called him from deep inside, but it felt as if other forces wanted to turn him back. Gritting his teeth, he wondered if this was a sign of things to come.

Almost faint with exhaustion, he had at last come through the storm. Now high up in the cold, clear air he saw sky again, and Elrilion. Beneath its light he made his crude camp; though little more than a blanket in the lee of an overhanging rock, and a far cry from the comforts of home, it would do. Oswain was tough and well trained in the rugged skills of outdoor life. As he lay, drifting into sleep, he recalled his parting from the palace. The king and queen had not questioned his going, nor the time nor the way, for it had long been known that he should go.

As long as he could remember Oswain had been taught that he must one day journey away from the comforts of the palace to perform a special mission that only he could do – though no one could tell him quite what it was. He remembered as a child asking his teacher about it.

'All in good time. All in good time,' he was told.

Oswain smiled at the memory. He had asked the same question year after year, and always received the same answer. But now, after twenty-one years, it seemed the time had come at last.

When he set out, his father, King Argil, had laid a firm hand on his shoulder and encouraged him to be brave. He was to send word when the task was done. His mother, Queen Talesanna, had gazed steadily into his eyes, her own grey eyes grave.

'Elmesh go with you, my son. Let your heart be strong, for I see not only enemies around you but a battle that shall take place within you. I shall pray and trust that you will conquer both.'

Then, with a quick kiss for his little sister, Princess Alena, he had left the security of the City of Elmar with as little fuss as a man going about his daily duties.

With a yawn he settled for the night. Tomorrow he would descend to the waste plains that preceded the forest.

*   *   *

Mrs Trotter was one of those extremely sensible folk who know just the right thing to do when they are worried. She didn't stand around wringing her hands. Instead, she stoked up the fire, put the kettle on and got Sarah to help her prepare something to eat. As a result, instead of everyone pacing the room in anxiety, they found them-selves sitting by a cosy fire, taking their fill of tea and crumpets, and before long feeling somewhat restored in spirits. Trotter especially was back to his old self.

'Before we attempt anything else,' he declared, 'we must have Gilmere repaired, for it was the only real weapon that we had.'

'But I thought it was too badly smashed to be mended,' said Andrew through a mouthful of crumpet. 'How could anyone fix that mess?' He indicated the pile of twisted metal and shattered glass in Trotter's handkerchief. 'I think I'd just throw it away.'

'Young man,' replied Trotter, 'you will one day learn that when a work of art is broken it should be returned to its creator. He will do with it what he can. He may decide it is beyond repair and scrap it, or else he may remake it; but that should be his decision, not yours or mine.' He smiled at Andrew's glum face. 'Don't be too upset, Andrew. We shall return Gilmere to Elmesh for such a ruling and hope that it will be repaired.' He glanced at the others. 'If you are ready, I will take you to the Enchanted Glade.'

Leaving Mrs Trotter to take care of the house, Trotter led the way with Aldred bringing up the rear and keeping a watchful eye open for danger. Andrew noticed that he was carrying a short sword. It was by now quite dark and Sarah and Andrew's eyes, not being as keen as those of the animals, were as good as useless as they stumbled blindly along the twisting path. It was only when they came to an occasional clearing that they managed to make out the shadowy shapes of the trees.

They had no idea how long the journey took or how deep into the forest they had gone. Indeed, after a while they lost all sense of their bearings and began to feel quite light-headed. Sarah fancied she could smell exotic

odours and heady scents, almost tropical in their
heaviness. Surely this could not still be the petrified
forest with its gloomy mosses and dormant branches?
They must have moved into some other realm altogether.

At that moment, the little group broke from the
undergrowth and came into the pale light of a starry
night. Before them loomed a mass of rock outlined
against the sky. The air around tingled with life and
mystery. They smelled sweet scents carried on a warm
breeze. Never had Sarah and Andrew felt so wonderfully
alive. Trotter didn't need to tell them that they had arrived
at the Enchanted Glade.

He led them through a narrow pass between two tall
stones. Before them, under the starlit sky, stretched a lush
clearing filled with a vast array of plants whose night-
muted blues and greens spread in all directions. Trotter
explained: 'However hard she tries, Hagbane cannot
discover the whereabouts of this place. You see, since she
stole the Merestone, a protection has fallen upon the
glade, and though she searches for it, she does so in vain.
It is the *source*, you understand. That is why things still
grow here as in the elder days. Her magic cannot reach it.
Now, come, I will take you to Elmere itself.'

Over to one side of the glade was a high overhanging
rock covered in grey-green moss. Beneath it lay a stone
shelf in which was set an oval pool about a metre across.
As they drew near it, their feelings of awareness grew
stronger and stronger and an intense happiness filled
their hearts to bursting point.

From the overhanging rock droplets of water formed
themselves like pearls and fell one by one with a bright
plip into the pool below. No dewdrop glistening in the

morning sun could match these droplets for silvery brilliance, for each, when it fell, glowed as if the light of Elrilion had been trapped within it. Luminous shadows flickered and darted about the glade from the watery jewels, and as they fell into the waiting pool, the water shone with their captured light. The faces of the children, as they gazed in wonder, were pale and ghostlike in the light of the limpid pool. Awe-struck, they said nothing.

'This is Elmere, the Star Pool, where the Merestone once lay,' whispered Trotter. 'Alas, that is no more but the pool still captures Elrilion's fire. It is also the origin of the mirror. We trust that what was created here can be recreated. Pass me the pieces, Aldred, if you will.'

The stoat obliged and, with great reverence, Trotter dropped the fragments into the water. A crackling sound, like the breaking of ice, accompanied his action and blue flashes of light flickered in the depths of the pool.

'There, it is done. That is all we can do here for tonight. But back at home we must have a proper council of war to determine our best course.' The badger spoke with fresh resolution, his eyes sparkling behind his spectacles. The feeling was shared by each of them, and, though reluctant to leave Elmere, they were almost dancing with excitement as they retraced their steps to Trotter's house. This time the children had no difficulty in seeing their way, even on the darkest stretches of the path.

4

Fumble, Mumble and Grumble

Back at the cottage they found a weasel awaiting them, whom Trotter introduced as Stiggle. He turned out to be Aldred's second-in-command and had come the moment news of the day's events had reached him. Mrs Trotter had told him all that had happened so far.

So, the council of war began, late in the evening, with the six huddled together around the fire, drinking steaming mugs of cocoa. Andrew stifled a yawn. It had been a long day and he felt like dozing off but no one was prepared to consider sleep just yet.

'It seems to me,' Trotter began, 'that our first object must be to rescue Peter from Hagbane's clutches. To do that we must discover his precise whereabouts in the castle dungeons, for that is where she will have taken him. Now, if you are correct, Aldred, and she somehow knew of the children's coming, you may be sure that she is hatching some evil plan, using Peter as a hostage. She will no doubt question him thoroughly as to who you children are. Now, Peter may be strong-willed but few can hide anything for long once she has them in her grip. So our rescue attempt needs to be soon.'

'Oh, this is just too awful,' Sarah cried. 'To think of that horrible old Shadow-witch hurting my brother. Why, it's evil! Can't we do something *now*? I mean, she may be questioning him and doing all sorts of terrible things.

Oh, *please*, let's not just sit here talking! I want to go and get him out.'

Aldred held up a paw. 'It's not as simple as that, Sarah. For one thing, the castle is heavily guarded by Grogs and Grims, and just to charge the walls would be fatal. Most of our folk are scared even to go near the place, let alone inside. No, we must use our cunning and trust that Peter is all right, at least for the moment. Assuming that's all there is to it,' he added with a knowing glance in Trotter's direction.

'I think you're being very unfair not trusting us,' exclaimed Sarah, who had noticed his look. 'I mean, do you really think that we're on her side or something?'

'I'm just a soldier,' Aldred replied. 'All I know is that you turned up out of the blue and that your brother went off with Hagbane, and our only good weapon is ruined because of him.'

Sarah was just about to have a go at the stoat when her brother intervened. 'Leave it, sis,' he said. 'It won't do any good. We've got to help Peter, and I want to do something tonight. It's no use getting into a row about whose side we're really on.'

Sarah huffed and folded her arms, glowering from beneath her lowered brows. She hated it when people didn't think she was telling the truth.

'I believe there are three forest-folk who could discover Peter's whereabouts for us and pass the word to him not to lose hope.'

All eyes turned on Stiggle, who had sat listening thus far.

'Who are they, Stiggle?' Trotter queried.

'Why, three who are small enough to escape the

guard's notice, sharp enough to find their way in and stupid enough not to be afraid. I'm thinking of Fumble, Mumble and Grumble.'

'Not those incompetent mice! You really must be joking,' exclaimed Aldred. 'Why, they can't even find their way out of their own nest without making a mess of it. Quite useless as fighting troops. I remember the time when . . .'

'Hold on, Aldred,' interrupted Trotter. 'Stiggle's idea is not bad. Unless, of course, you have a better one.'

Aldred thought for a moment. 'No, I don't,' he admitted. 'But let's face it, it's a bit risky, sir.'

'Risky or not, we've got to take a chance if we are to reach Peter at all. If we are to succeed, any rescue attempt will have to be made without a hitch and that means we must know where he is, and he must expect us. As far as I can see these three mice are our best hope.'

Aldred agreed with some reluctance, while Sarah and Andrew were just glad that something was being done. So it was decided that Stiggle should fetch the three mice.

*   *   *

The spell that Hagbane had cast over Peter wore off within sight of her castle and he came to himself with a start of horror as the vision of loveliness transformed into the vile form of the Shadow-witch. He realised, too, that there was no shiny mountain bike. Instead, his arms were pinioned to his sides by the painful grip of two reptilian creatures that he later found out were called Grogs, and who marched him along behind Hagbane as she strode back to her lair. Peter felt sick from the stench of his captors and couldn't bring himself even to look at their faces.

His heart sank even lower when he saw the gaunt stone fortress with its tall turrets and grim battlements. This was no pretty fairy castle but a place of dread where even the dark slit windows seemed to have eyes. The Grogs dragged him into the gloomy portal and a massive, iron-studded oak door swung noiselessly open at Hagbane's command, though no doorkeeper could be seen. Peter shuddered. His captors marched him across an open courtyard and into a large bare room, where he was flung to the floor. The evil Shadow-witch towered over him, full of menace, and not quite solid, like a huge dark and brooding ghost constantly changing shape before his eyes.

'So, what strange creature do we have here!' she grated. 'Who are you? What is your name, man-child? Answer me now, or I'll make it very uncomfortable for you.'

'Please, my name is Peter Brown,' he replied, thinking that it would be best to tell her the truth. 'I don't really know what I'm doing here, except that I came in through a hole in an oak tree.'

At this the Shadow-witch's eyes gleamed. 'The old oak tree, eh? I have heard tell of this, and I do not like it. Nor do I believe you are telling me all you know. Who sent you? Why have you come to the Great Forest – into *my* domain? Eh? Answer me now!'

'Well, nobody sent us, as far as I know . . .' began Peter,

feeling afraid, for he knew his answer would displease the Shadow-witch.

'Liar!' she spat, and kicked him hard in the ribs with her pointed shoe. Peter gasped with the pain and tears came to his eyes.

'Please, it's the truth. I don't know how we got into this. All I know is what Trotter has . . . has told us.' His mouth dropped in dismay as he realised that he had said too much.

'So there is more? I thought so. What has that meddling old fool of a badger been up to this time?'

But Peter had made up his mind. He would not betray his friends. His mouth was firmly closed.

'Stubborn, eh? Well, if you want to do it the hard way, that's fine by me. I can wait. Guards, take him away! A night in the dungeons will loosen your tongue – and if it doesn't, I have other, more painful ways. Think about it carefully. You will be chained up without food or water until you decide to speak.'

The Grogs dragged him down a steep flight of stone stairs into an underground dungeon. One of them lit a lantern, and then they propelled him along a foul-smelling corridor. In the flickering light he saw many wretched animals caged up and some groaned as he passed. His guards pushed him into a grimy cell and tied his wrists tightly to a ring on the wall above his head so that he was stretched up on tiptoe. The door slammed shut with a dull clang and Peter was left in the darkness. His arms were already beginning to ache as the first wave of despair swept over him.

*   *   *

'Get out of my way, you great drip!'

The speaker was Grumble and thus he announced the arrival of the three mice in Trotter's front room. He was addressing Fumble who had just trodden on his foot and poked an elbow in his ribs in the process of getting through the door.

'Wassamarrawithyouoo, gnarrasar.' The third member of the trio was the incoherent Mumble.

'These three are aptly named,' laughed Trotter. 'And I don't think I need to tell you who is who. Fumble, Mumble and Grumble, I want you to meet Sarah and Andrew Brown. Alas, I would have liked to be able to introduce Peter as well, but . . . well, more of that in a minute.'

Fumble reached out a paw to shake Sarah's hand, but somehow his arms and legs got mixed up and he finished up in a tangled heap at her feet. 'Hello,' he grinned. 'Sorry about that. It must be the uneven floor.'

Sarah laughed, and liked him.

'Goo evn'in nicetermetyer,' mumbled Mumble to Andrew.

'Why don't you speak up, you dimwit?' bellowed Grumble. 'Good evening, both of you. Although I don't think it is at all good at the moment. A fine to-do this is, getting me out of bed with these two idiots. It had better be something important, that's all I can say. Anyway, here we are!'

Andrew glanced at Aldred who gave him one of those 'don't-say-I-didn't-warn-you' shrugs. The children were beginning to see his point, for these really were the most unlikely spies imaginable. Even saying hello seemed to cause a minor catastrophe. Trotter, however, was quite unmoved by all of it.

'Now, you three mice, I have a very important and dangerous mission that I wish you to undertake for us and for which, Elmesh only knows why, you are the only ones suitable.

'Hagbane has captured Peter, the brother of these two, who are Children of Time Beyond Time, and is at present holding him in her castle. We want you to find your way in and to discover his whereabouts. Assuming you can do this,' (at this point Aldred gave a snort) 'I want you to pass on the message that he is to be ready for a rescue attempt. Many die for lack of hope in that accursed place, so it is extremely important that you encourage him to hold on. Is that understood?'

Mumble muttered something incomprehensible which the rest took to mean yes.

'Once you have found Peter,' Trotter continued, 'I want you to spy out the land and find the easiest way for us to get to him, if there is one. You must return to us with that information as soon as possible. We will then plan our rescue attempt.'

'Fat lot of hope I've got of even reaching the castle with these two, let alone returning,' complained Grumble. 'But we'll do it for you, Trotter, if you say so. Though I don't like it one little bit,' he added.

Fumble, presumably intending to make some sort of speech, stretched out his hand. Unfortunately, he succeeded only in knocking over a vase of dried grasses that stood on the table. Mrs Trotter shrieked as it crashed to the floor.

'My best vase!'

Trotter groaned and Aldred lifted his paws in despair.

'Go now,' he exclaimed, 'before you do any more damage. And good luck, because you certainly look as though you're going to need it!'

* * *

The three mice crouched outside the castle walls. In spite of Fumble falling into a stream on the way and tripping over countless tree roots, and Grumble's continual complaints at fate for having given him such companions, nobody had noticed their approach. Not surprisingly, Mumble was the quietest of all.

'Now we need to find a way in,' whispered Fumble.

'Brilliant,' replied Grumble. 'Go to the top of the class!'

Mumble murmured something.

'What's that? Speak clearly for once, can't you?' yelled Grumble.

'Shush.'

They saw then that Mumble was pointing to a water waste-pipe.

'That'll do. Well done, Mumble,' said Fumble. 'Well, what are we waiting for? Come on. Shall I lead?'

'Oh no,' Grumble replied firmly. 'You'll come last. It's safer that way!'

After some effort they found their way through to the other end of the pipe and discovered that it drained the floor of the castle washroom. Luckily, nobody had decided to pour any water away while they were climbing up it. They were inside the dimly lit and evil-smelling lair of Hagbane. Very quietly (even Fumble was careful) they crept around the draughty corridors looking for any sign of Peter. For a long time they found nothing and it was just as they were beginning to despair of ever finding him that Fumble had his lucky accident.

They were passing a floor-level window covered with an iron grating when Fumble slipped on some candle grease or tripped over a flagstone (afterwards nobody was sure which) and fell through the grating into the room below. Grumble was leading at the time and Mumble, who saw what had happened, muttered something that sounded like, 'He's filing down the widow.'

Grumble was just about to shout at Mumble when they heard Fumble call out from down below.

'I think I've found him. Down here.'

Sure enough, he was right. They had stumbled upon the basement dungeon where Peter was imprisoned. Without further delay the other two mice jumped down to join Fumble. They saw a dark figure tied to the wall.

'Psst. Are you Peter?' asked Grumble.

'Y-y-yes. W-w-who are you?' Peter answered through chattering teeth, for by now he was numb with cold.

'Never mind that for now. We're from Trotter, and that's all you need to know. We've been sent to find you and to tell you that help is on its way. So don't be afraid, because you'll soon be out of here. Is there anything we can do?'

'Y-y-yes. Th-there is. C-c-can you untie my wrists? I don't think I can last out much longer.'

The three mice scrabbled up Peter's legs and up his arms – which was an odd sensation to say the least – and began to gnaw at his bonds. It seemed to take ages and ages, especially as Fumble kept falling off and had to keep climbing back up again. However, at last it was done. The ropes gave and Peter collapsed onto the floor in an exhausted heap.

'Oh, thank you, thank you,' he gasped and, to his shame, he began to cry. Actually, as it usually does, crying made him feel much better, and he soon pulled himself together.

'I'm sorry about that,' he said. 'But I've made such a mess of things. Are they really going to be able to rescue me? I honestly thought I'd be left here to die.'

'Yes, of course they'll get you out,' declared Grumble with somewhat more confidence than he actually felt. 'Trotter can do most things. Why, you know, he once saved my life when a Grog was chasing me and had me in a corner. So I'm sure he'll help you. We'll be back soon, so be ready.'

Mumble muttered his assent and Peter looked puzzled.

'Oh, don't worry about him,' explained Fumble. 'He never speaks clearly, but then he never says anything very important anyway.'

Before a hurt-looking Mumble could protest, Grumble dragged them away.

'Come on, you two, we've still got to find a way for the others to get in. That drainpipe won't do. Look after yourself, Peter. We'll return as soon as possible.'

With that they were off, leaving Peter feeling very much better. As they left, Fumble tripped several times and brought the other two crashing down on top of him at least once. For the first time that day, Peter laughed. Then he winced as pins and needles set into his hands.

5

To the Rescue!

Knowing that they could do nothing until the three mice returned, which might take some time, the company at Trotter's house decided to get some sleep. Fortunately, there were plenty of spare beds since the house was often used as a place of refuge for forest-folk who were fleeing from Hagbane's troops.

Sarah snuggled down into a bed of hay and sheep's wool. She gave a deep sigh. It had been an exciting and disturbing day, and a very long one. Exhausted by the events, she soon fell asleep and for a while she slept deeply. Later, she began to dream. . . .

She was climbing a great tree and it seemed to go up for ever. Her legs ached as she clambered upwards into the night sky – up towards a white star that glowed in the distance. Yet however long she climbed it was always too far away. At length, so tired, she slipped, and began to fall.

Down she tumbled until she was rolling and bouncing down a long flight of dark stairs. Faces flashed before her as she fell – Trotter, Aldred, Andrew, Peter, Hagbane – each shattered into a thousand pieces before her gaze like the smashed reflection of a broken mirror. On she fell, into the never-ending darkness.

At last, she landed with a bump and found herself walking in the Enchanted Glade. The pool seemed to beckon her and she ran towards it. She gazed deep into its waters, expecting to see her own reflection. With a shock that made her catch her breath, she saw, not herself, but the face of a man staring blankly back at her. Before she could recover from the fright, flames consumed the entire image. Then the glade was on fire, and the forest. Fire ran along the branches of the trees until everything was a sheet of flames. Sarah screamed and saw Sam Squirrel writhing in Hagbane's grip. Then she saw Peter's face and awoke with a start.

She lay for a while breathing rapidly in the pale light of early morning.

'Thank goodness it's only a dream,' she said to herself. 'But then, supposing it's trying to tell me something?'

Quietly, she got up and crept from the house. The grey dawn made the forest look even more mournful and she shivered with the cold. Somehow she seemed to know which way to go – a turn to the right here, left there, under this branch, across these rocks; unerringly she followed her instincts until she came once again to the mysterious splendour of the Enchanted Glade.

She hesitated now, the dream still vivid in her mind. Fear and doubt possessed her and she felt no desire to gaze into Elmere. Reluctantly, she made herself approach the bowl, her heart thudding uncomfortably, and steeling herself she peered into the shining water. There she saw her own reflection. A mixture of relief mingled with disappointment flooded over her. She looked again – and this time she saw the mirror, Gilmere, lying perfectly whole in the bottom of the shallow pool. Gingerly, she reached her hand into the cold water and slowly withdrew it.

'Ah, so you have found it, have you?'

The deep voice from behind made her jump with fright, so that she almost dropped the precious mirror back into the water. The back of her neck tingled as slowly she turned to face whoever it was.

'Trotter!' She gasped his name with relief. 'Oh, you frightened me! I didn't hear you coming.'

The badger smiled his apologies. 'Forgive me, my dear, but I followed you here. It is as well to be on the safe side in these days.' He glanced at the object in her hand. 'I see that Gilmere is made well again. That is truly good news for us, for I do not doubt that we shall need its power today. Now come quickly, child, for if I am not very much mistaken, those incredible mice should be back with news by now.'

When they got back they found everybody up and about, with Mrs Trotter busily supplying hot toast and marmalade. The three mice were eagerly reporting their good news. Not only had they found Peter but they had also discovered a little-used side entrance that led through a tunnel to the kitchens and dungeons. All this took some time to relate, mostly because Mumble kept adding incomprehensible bits of information through a mouthful of toast and everyone had to keep saying 'Pardon?' or 'Could you repeat that, please?' However, all were very excited and cheered by the news and by the fact that the mirror was repaired. So, as soon as breakfast was over, they prepared to launch Operation Rescue, as Andrew called it.

'I don't think we should send too many,' said Trotter. 'There's no sense in drawing attention to ourselves more than we have to.'

'I want to go,' said Sarah firmly.

'So do I,' Andrew added.

So, after further discussion, it was agreed that the

mice, the children and Stiggle would make up the rescue party while Trotter and Aldred would station themselves outside the castle to deal with any pursuers once Peter was out.

Following Mumble, who by common agreement was the quietest, the party came within sight of the Shadow-witch's castle. The fortress stood in a clearing but gorse bushes grew quite thickly to a distance of about seventy-five metres from the wall on the eastern side and this provided good cover.

'Quietly now,' cautioned Stiggle. 'There are bound to be guards about.'

They crept through the undergrowth until Mumble raised a hand for them to stop.

'There's the entrance,' whispered Grumble, pointing to a round doorway that was obviously the opening to an upward sloping corridor. 'There are a couple of gates that we'll have to break through once we're inside but at least we'll be under cover.'

'We'll have to take a chance and run across that open space,' said Stiggle. 'If you're ready, I'll go first.'

They all nodded and he shot out from the undergrowth, making for the doorway. However, he had crossed no more than halfway when there was a loud roar and a huge and fearsome Grog stepped out from the shadow of the walls.

'Stop where you are!' he commanded, pointing his spear at Stiggle's heart. 'One move and you're dead, vermin scum.'

He advanced on the poor weasel and prodded him in the throat with the spear. 'What are you up to, you filth, and who else is with you?' he snarled.

Before Stiggle could reply, Sarah stepped boldly from the bushes, clutching Gilmere in her hand.

'Over here,' she cried.

The Grog span round to face her.

'Well now, here's a pretty catch and no mistake. Mistress Hagbane *will* be interested.'

He took a pace towards her and, at that very moment, Sarah flipped open the mirror and pointed it towards him. A blinding beam of light blazed from the mirror, as triumphant and terrible as the sun in its brilliance. She snapped the lid shut and blinked. The Grog was nowhere to be seen.

'Oh dear. I've killed him!' cried Sarah. 'I didn't mean to do that.' She suddenly felt very sick.

'No you haven't,' laughed Stiggle. 'Look, he's turned into a frog!'

Indeed, a very frightened frog was hopping away into the bushes just as fast as his legs could carry him.

'Grogs into frogs,' Andrew chortled. 'Whatever next? That's some flashlight.'

They quickly gained the shadowy entrance to the tunnel that led into the castle. Their next obstacle was an iron gate about ten metres along the corridor. This resisted all their efforts to open it in spite of there being no obvious lock.

'Here, let me have a go with that mirror,' demanded Andrew as he snatched it from Sarah's hands. 'I'll melt it down or turn it into a metal frog, perhaps. You watch!'

He opened the mirror but, although the same radiance blazed out, the door remained completely unaffected.

'Huh! That's not much good, is it? Looks like it can only do one trick a day.'

It was Stiggle who spoke to Andrew. 'I think it's not Gilmere that is at fault, but you. Nobody shows off with Elmesh's gifts: it's not given for you to do tricks with but to serve the cause of good. Now, Sarah, I think you have more idea. Take the mirror, will you?'

Sarah obeyed and directed the blazing light at the gate. 'Gate fast closed by Hagbane's might, Open up to Gilmere's light.'

At once the door flew open and they passed through unhindered. Andrew looked suitably shame-faced and had the grace to say sorry to Stiggle.

'That was a bit silly of me, I suppose. Trust my older sister to get it right!'

Nothing more was said about the matter and they encountered no further obstacles until they came at last to the outer door of the dungeons. This also gave way to Sarah's use of Gilmere and the children stumbled forwards through the gloom until the mice stopped them outside Peter's cell. Peter blinked in the mirror's sudden light as his cell door swung open.

'Andrew, Sarah. You've made it! Thank goodness. And the mice. Fantastic!'

The children gave each other big thankful hugs.

'We're so glad to see you alive,' said Andrew. 'Are you all right?'

'Yes, thanks to these mice, otherwise I'd have been very uncomfortable by now. She tied me up to that ring on the wall, you know.'

'The wicked old bat,' declared Sarah. 'Just wait till we get her.'

'Well not just yet,' said Stiggle. 'We must get out first.' He quickly introduced himself. 'Hello, Peter, my name's

Stiggle. I'm Aldred's second-in-command.'

Peter clasped his paw. 'It's really good to meet you, Stiggle. Yes, you're dead right. I don't want to stay here a moment longer. Come on!'

'What about the other prisoners here, the forest-folk?' asked Andrew. 'Can't we get some of them out?'

Grumble was just about to say that he wondered if there would be enough time when their questions were answered for them. A key grated in the lock of the main door up the stairs.

'Quick, run for it! Run for your lives!' shouted Stiggle.

* * *

Hagbane had not slept that night. All through the dark hours she had paced to and fro in her den, muttering to herself, planning and plotting. This strange creature in her dungeon was a difficult problem; he was obviously from *outside*. True, she had worked out that something was up and had very cleverly caught him. The question was, what to do now? Should she kill him? Then he would die with his secrets. Well, she would get those out of him in the morning. Yet that still left the others. And were they the only ones? There was more to this than met the eye. She brooded over the matter for many long hours.

As soon as it was light, she hurried to her spell-room, an evil-smelling place filled with jars containing mysterious and horrible substances and shelves lined with dusty brown books of magic. In one corner lay an object covered with a velvet cloth. Gloating like a miser with his gold, she removed the covering to reveal the object of her desire: the Merestone of the Great Forest of Alamore. It glowed faintly in the gloom of the den as she gazed upon it with her greedy eyes.

'While this is mine I have nothing to fear,' she murmured to herself. 'And it *is* mine, all mine. With this I shall rule for ever. No one can touch me. I shall be the greatest queen in all the universe.' Her voice rose to a screech as she stretched out her gnarled hands in a gesture of defiance against the whole world and everybody in it. 'Mine! It's all *mine!*'

She covered the jewel, her eyes burning with desire. With a swirl of her cloak she turned to the bookshelves, from which she removed an old volume. Hastily turning the pages, she came across an ancient script.

From the far West he shall come, a man sent to deliver.
By the children of time beyond time shall his path be marked.
To set the ancient stone within its rightful sphere; to bring to
life again to the land of desolation, to. . . .

Hagbane spat and screeched. 'I must question the prisoner. He must know about this. I'll get it out of him. Guards!'

A sleepy Grog came running at her cry. He stood shakily to attention.

'Fetch the prisoner at once,' she ordered. 'And be quick about it or I shall turn you into a toad and boil you alive!'

She paced up and down waiting his return, twisting her fingers and smacking the palm of her hand with a clenched fist. At length the guard returned and burst breathlessly through the door.

'E's gone, yer 'ighness. Escaped down the tunnel. I don't know 'ow it could 'ave 'appened.'

'What!'

'I think they've only just gone, ma'am. Shall we get after them?'

'No, you fool. I shall handle this myself!'

She strode grim-faced from the room and began to climb the steps that led to the top of the tower from where she could view the surrounding forest.

The company, meanwhile, had rushed from the gateway in the wall and darted for the undergrowth. Stiggle was fastest away. The children had to go more slowly because Peter was quite weak and stiff. The mice stayed with them but made matters worse because Fumble succeeded in tripping everyone over so that they became hopelessly entangled on the ground. They were still in full view of the castle.

'You stupid twit!' exclaimed Grumble. 'I've never seen anyone . . .'

He was interrupted by a shrill screech from the castle walls. They turned to see Hagbane standing on top of the tower with her arms stretched out to the sky, holding two long rods. She looked a terrifying sight, rising up like a dark, brooding storm cloud from the castle ramparts.

'Run for it,' shouted Peter. 'Never mind me.'

A chilling cold blast hit them as they ran, numbing them to the bone. Thunder crashed and black lightning crackled from Hagbane's wands. Snow began to fall heavily; the wind blew up and moments later they were caught in the midst of a fierce blizzard in which they soon lost all sense of direction. It was as though they had been plunged into an instant Arctic winter.

Struggling knee-deep through the snow, half-blinded, they grew wearier and wearier until it was almost impossible to lift their leaden limbs through the biting cold.

'I don't think I can go on,' gasped Peter. 'You must keep moving. Save yourselves.'

'No, we must stick together,' Andrew cried above the howl of the wind. 'Pick up those mice, Sarah, or they'll be buried alive.'

'That's what'll happen to us all,' she groaned. 'I feel so sleepy . . . so sleepy . . . must rest. . . .'

With that, Sarah collapsed in a heap in the driving snow. The last thing she heard was a shrill shriek of laughter echoing across the snow from the castle tower. Then everything went black.

6

The Wizards' Sacrifice

'We must get shelter,' gasped Peter as he and his brother tried to lift Sarah. 'Look, let's try to get to that tree over there.'

He indicated a spreading sycamore tree that was not so badly affected by the snow. It took a terrific effort but with much puffing and panting they managed to drag Sarah to its shelter.

'Round this side, Pete. It's out of the wind and there's no snow.'

Once they were safely in the lee of the sycamore they began to feel better, and Sarah stirred.

'Where am I?' she groaned. 'What's happening? Oh, my head!'

'It's all right now, Sarah. You're safe,' Peter reassured her as he hugged her to himself. 'I think we've beaten that old Shadow-witch's trick after all. It's certainly nice to be free again, anyway.'

'Where's Stiggle, and the mice?'

'The mice are here with us. It looks like Stiggle got away. He's fast,' Peter explained. 'I expect he'll fetch Trotter and Aldred to help us back.'

Sarah smiled with relief as Andrew leapt to his feet and began to prance about laughing.

'Yah, silly old bat! Can't stop us. We're the great. . . .'

He never finished. At that moment, without any

warning, everything went topsy-turvy. The ground beneath them gave way and all six found themselves tumbling in a crazy tangle of earth, roots and helpless bodies. Down and down they slithered until finally they landed in a heap at the bottom of a deep pit.

'Ooo! Ouch! Ow! What's happened?'

'Is everyone all right?'

'Is this my leg?'

'No, it's mine!'

'Oh, sorry!'

'Get your foot out of my ear.'

'I can't. I'm stuck under somebody's bottom.'

'Yeuk! I've just got a mouthful of earth.'

After much struggling and groaning, the six of them managed to disentangle themselves and take stock of their situation, which didn't seem to be too bright. They had fallen about three metres down a narrow hole and there seemed to be no way the children could climb out.

Peter shook the earth off his clothes. 'Well, we're in a right fix now, aren't we? It's just a miracle we're all OK. We might have had all sorts of injuries.' He peered upwards and frowned. 'I haven't a clue how we're going to get out of here.'

'Do you think it's another of Hagbane's tricks?' Sarah enquired.

'Who knows?' he shrugged. He was beginning to wish he had never suggested climbing the oak tree in the first place. It seemed that nothing had gone right ever since they had arrived.

'Here, wait a minute, everyone,' Andrew called with excitement. 'Look, there's a tunnel here. It got half covered in by the earth when we fell.'

They turned and saw Andrew vanish into a small hole.

'Hey, you can stand up in here,' his voice boomed. 'It must lead somewhere. Are you coming?'

'Probably back to Hagbane's castle,' moaned Grumble.

'No, it's going in the opposite direction, I'm sure,' said Peter. 'Let's try it. It might just lead us out. Let's face it, we've got to do something.'

What he said made sense so, very cautiously, they began to follow Andrew along the underground passage. It was so dark that they had to hold on to one another and feel their way along the earth walls.

'It's a bit scary, isn't it?' Sarah whispered.

'Yes, but at least it's warm and dry.'

'And away from Hagbane.'

'We hope.'

'Oh, don't say that.'

'Sh, there's a light ahead.'

They halted, bumping into one another. Fumble got himself wrapped around Mumble's legs.

'Gerrof. Ahfortyer wera spida!'

'Quiet, you two,' ordered Peter. 'Let's go carefully now.'

The pale yellow glow was still a long way off and it took them quite a time to reach it. Everyone had lost track of how long they had been underground but their stomachs told them that it was well past lunch time. Eventually, they reached a left turn in the tunnel and it was from round this corner that the light came. Hearts thumping loudly, the company halted and with great caution six heads peered around to see what was awaiting them.

What they saw was not very much. Just a fairly large

underground chamber lit by burning torches set in brackets on the walls. The flickering light cast long shadows behind them as they emerged into the room.

'I wonder what this place is?' Peter asked.

'Well, it must belong to somebody,' answered Sarah. 'The question is, who?'

'Good afternoon.'

The voice was smooth and low and it almost made them jump out of their skins. Sarah stifled a scream. Huddling together, they turned to face its owner.

Before them stood two of the most bizarre characters any of them had ever seen. The taller one was a gaunt figure with hard features and a leering mouth. He possessed a straggly black beard and moustache and wore a silken scarlet robe covered with a mysterious yellow design. His partner, who was very short, reminded Andrew of an egg, for he was a fat, round creature, totally bald, and with apparently no neck. His robe of green silk was also covered in a curious pattern. He smiled a bland, oily smile and continued in his smooth low voice.

'Good afternoon. Did we startle you? I am most sorry. Welcome to our humble abode.' He raised an eyebrow. 'May I ask to whom we owe this pleasure?'

For a moment, nobody spoke. It was, unfortunately, Mumble who recovered his voice first.

'Gooafnun. Weforsfolkavcomfromagbinscastwerwis-cape.'

Their hosts looked puzzled.

'Oh, shut up, cloth-head,' snapped Grumble. 'Why do you even bother? I'm sorry about that,' he addressed the strange creatures. 'What he's trying to say is that we are forest-folk and we have just escaped from Hagbane's castle. We accidentally fell into your tunnel trying to hide from a snowstorm. We're very sorry about that and don't want to inconvenience you, so, if you will kindly show us the way out, we'll be off.'

'Not so fast,' the taller one spoke for the first time. His voice grated hard and Sarah gave a slight shiver. 'How do we know this is true?' he continued. 'How do we know you are not friends of Hagbane come to spy on us? Who are these strange beings, anyway?' He indicated the children.

Peter spoke up. 'Please, sirs, my name is Peter Brown and this is my brother, Andrew, and my sister, Sarah. We've come from a long way away and all we really want to do is to get back to our friends. So, if you don't mind, we would be ever so grateful if you could show us the way out.'

'Quite, quite,' said the short one. He glanced at his partner. 'Only it is a fair journey to the exit and you all look very tired and dirty. And, I should think, hungry and thirsty as well. Won't you stay and have a small meal before you go?'

The mention of food and drink made them all aware of their stomachs, especially Peter, who, of course, had not eaten or drunk since they first came to Trotter's cottage.

'Well, um, yes. Yes, thank you. That really is very kind of you. Only you will let us go soon, won't you?' he said.

'But of course,' replied the short one smoothly. 'Now we must introduce ourselves. My name is Sorda, and this is my colleague, Terras. We are, um, what you might call explorers, delving into the realms of knowledge, trying to understand the secrets of the earth and the heavens.'

'Oh, what we call scientists, then,' interjected Andrew.

'Scientists? Why, yes. Yes indeed. Scientists. Now come this way, please.'

They were led through a door into another much larger underground chamber. Peter glanced round. Drawings and strange instruments littered a bench in the middle of the room, and rolls of yellowed parchments and books lined shelves on three of the walls. A sour smell of chemicals and decay hung in the atmosphere. Almost at once Peter wished he had not accepted the invitation. It reminded him too much of Hagbane's castle.

Fumble tripped over something under the table and gasped with horror when he saw that it was a dead mouse. Lying on his back he looked up to see a whole string of mice hanging by their tails under the bench. He shivered and decided to stay well out of the way, and to keep an eye on things.

'Come and sit by the fire.' Terras' invitation was more like an order and the children obeyed with reluctance.

They sat, rigid with tension, before the blaze, saying nothing, until Sorda returned with a jug of steaming liquid and several metal goblets.

'Comfrey tea,' he beamed. 'Most thirst-quenching and refreshing.'

The children watched with suspicion as he filled the goblets and they waited until Terras and Sorda began to drink before savouring the brew themselves. But Sarah just pretended to drink hers by holding it to her mouth without taking any in.

Andrew and Peter both stared into the fire – and then the room began to spin. They tried to stand but found their legs wouldn't hold them. Faster and faster the room

span until first Peter and then Andrew slumped un-
conscious to the floor.

'What have you done?' Sarah shrieked as she saw her
brothers pass out. 'You've drugged them, haven't you?'

She was furious, and stood to face the two wizards (for
that is what they surely were) with her fists clenched and
her jaw set. Grumble and Mumble dashed to her side as,
eyes gleaming, their captors advanced towards her.

'Gilmere. Use Gilmere,' Grumble hissed from the side
of his mouth.

'Oh! I've given it back to Peter.'

Sarah made a dash for her brother but before she could
make it Terras pounced upon her and pinned her to the
floor. The two mice leapt in, followed by Sorda, who
grabbed them both and banged their heads together so
hard that they were stunned. He dropped their limp
bodies on the ground and turned to his henchman.

'Tie those four up,' ordered Terras from where he still
held Sarah captive. 'We'll use them for experiments later.
We'll make this girl the sacrifice for tonight. What a
stroke of luck, eh?'

Sorda gave a sinister laugh as he bound Grumble and
Mumble with cord. 'Yes, this should get us nicely into
Hagbane's favour and please her Grims. By the way,
weren't there three mice?'

'Yes. The other one must be somewhere about. But no
matter. We'll get him later. Let's deal with this one first.'

Sarah struggled and screamed as they hauled her to
her feet.

'Why are you doing this?' she sobbed. 'Please let us go.
We haven't done you any harm.'

Sorda smiled. 'Foolish child. Did you really think we

would let such an opportunity pass? We told you we experimented in all kinds of matters, and here you are, creatures we have never seen before. We shall use your brothers in our studies, and the mice too. But you, my dear, are going to be offered as a sacrifice to Hagbane's Grims. That way we shall keep her happy as well.'

'No. No!' Sarah struggled in their iron grip as they pulled her up a short flight of stairs to a wooden door. Opening it, they led her outside where before them stretched a long stone staircase, each step covered in strange symbols. It was by now late afternoon and the sun was setting as, slowly, the two evil wizards dragged her up the steps. A cold breeze blew across the darkening forest.

At length, in spite of Sarah's struggles, they reached a high stone platform at the summit of the staircase that now stretched like a grey, corrugated ribbon below them down to the yellow glare of the doorway. They lashed ropes tightly to Sarah's wrists and tied her arms above her head to two pillars on either side. Sorda drew a slender wand from the folds of his cloak and touched torches affixed to each post. Instantly they burst into flames and the two wizards chuckled as they watched their victim writhe in the flickering light.

'Heh, heh. The more she struggles, the more appetising she will be!' gloated Terras.

Hearing this, Sarah ceased struggling at once. She would give no pleasure to her wicked captors, she decided.

They turned and began to descend the steps, leaving her in the gathering gloom under the flitting light of the blazing torches. She cried. She shouted. But nobody came. The door below closed with a dull *thunk* and, alone and helpless, Sarah awaited her fate.

Fumble had, of course, seen all this from his hiding place under the table. He had not been idle. His first task had been to gnaw through the cords that bound his fellow-mice, who were just coming round.

'They're going to sacrifice Sarah to the Grims.' He spoke urgently to his dazed companions. 'We must get Peter and Andrew awake.'

They staggered across to the collapsed forms of the boys.

'Water. Let's try water,' said Grumble.

Quickly they found a bucket and, using the goblets, began to splash the lads with water.

'Wassamarra?' groaned Andrew. 'Ugh!'

'Wake up,' urged Fumble. 'They're going to kill Sarah.'

'What?' It was Peter who spoke first. 'Kill Sarah?'

Both boys retched and were violently sick.

'Ugh! That's better. What happened? The last thing I remember was having a drink. Then everything started spinning. . . .'

'You were drugged,' interrupted Fumble. 'Now Sarah's in great danger. We must stop those wizards.'

'Too late!'

They whirled round to see the two wizards standing at the doorway. Sorda locked the heavy door and together he and Terras strode down the staircase to where the boys and the mice cowered.

'You are too late,' continued Terras with a triumphant leer. 'She will die and so shall you.'

His callousness cleared Peter's head more effectively than the cold water.

'We'll see about that,' he cried and, leaping aside, drew

Gilmere from his pocket. With a press of the clasp it sprang open and living light gushed forth like a jet of golden water from a powerful hose. Saturated with such intense light, books and parchments burst into flames under its glare. A crystal ball exploded into a thousand fragments. Apparatus began to melt into smouldering heaps.

'Taste Elmesh's fire!' Peter shouted.

The wizards screeched with rage but fled in fear into the tunnel as they saw the fury on Peter's face and the destruction he was wreaking.

'Now for Sarah.'

They rushed the flight of stairs and reached the locked door.

'This time I'll do it right,' muttered Peter. 'By the light of Elmesh, let this door be broken. Let this door be broken!'

At once, to the sound of splintering wood, the oak door shattered into firewood before the blazing light. They were outside. Ahead of them stretched the long stone staircase where they could see the distant figure of Sarah in the torchlight. They rushed up the stairs as fast as their still-shaking legs could carry them.

'Don't worry, we're coming, Sarah,' called Andrew breathlessly.

At that very moment a shrill screech pierced the night sky. They gazed in the direction from which it had come and saw a black dot that, even as they watched, grew rapidly in size as it plummeted towards them. Down it shot at unbelievable speed, a mighty bird with powerful wings and outstretched talons glinting in the flames from the wizards' den. Eyes glaring, it streaked straight towards the helpless Sarah.

Before they could react to this horror, three other cries rent the air. They turned in dismay to see other dark shapes speeding on great black wings towards the sacrificial victim from the direction of Hagbane's castle.

'Quickly, quickly!' screamed Sarah. 'Help me. Please, please help me!'

7

Battle in the Sky

Peter and Andrew were halfway up the steep steps, lungs bursting and legs aching with the effort, but it was too late. The outspread wings of the giant bird, which they now saw to be a white eagle, seemed to fill the sky above Sarah. Tears of frustration and defeat choked Peter. His own sister was about to be torn to pieces! Desperately, he reached into his pocket for Gilmere.

But instead of clutching Sarah in those fearsome talons, the eagle landed beside her and tore at her bonds until she was free. Nearly faint with terror and unable to hold herself up any longer, the exhausted girl collapsed to the ground.

Peter, almost at the top of the stairs by now, seized his chance and flicked Gilmere open, pointing it in desperation. A blaze of light banished the gloom and struck the bird full on, but the eagle seemed to grow larger and brighter in its glare. His feathers shimmered with a silvery sheen but nothing further happened. There was no burning, no destruction. The panting would-be-rescuers stood amazed and beaten.

Then the bird spoke. His voice was harsh and cawing and full of authority.

'I am Arca, envoy of Elmesh. I see the glory of Gilmere is come too. It is well – but you do no good by shining it upon one who shares its nature. Close it, Peter Brown, for

69

you reveal too much by its light.'

Dumbfounded, and after a moment's hesitation, Peter did as he was bidden. Except for the flickering torches that cast eerie shadows all around them, all was dark. Arca spoke once more.

'Now there is little time, for the enemy has smelt blood. It is Sarah they desire, though you are all in great danger. I will take her to safety and deal with the foe, but you must flee for your lives. Down the steps you will find a path to the left. It leads to the river where you will find a boat. Look now, the enemy comes!'

Above them wheeled three bat-like creatures of such enormous size that they looked like prehistoric monsters. At an unseen signal they swooped towards their target.

'On my back, Sarah,' commanded Arca as she struggled to her feet. 'Quickly now, the rest of you. Run!'

Peter pushed the mirror into Sarah's hands. 'Here, take this and use it,' he panted. 'And look after yourself.'

Sarah clambered onto the eagle's neck as he bent low. As soon as she was astride, the mighty wings swished the air and with Sarah clinging on for dear life he soared aloft.

For a moment, the others stood in awe gazing after the eagle, but the sight of a Grim diving towards them jerked each one back to reality.

'Come on,' yelled Peter. 'Run for it!'

Down the steps they raced, feeling a cold rush of wind as the Grim, with its talons bared, swooped low over their heads. For once, Fumble was a help because he tripped over the other two mice and they tumbled together to the bottom of the steps in record time. Not that Grumble was very impressed.

'You stupid mouse,' he cried. 'Why can't you ever look

where you're going?'

'Mmmggh,' agreed Mumble.

'Oh, shut up!'

Before a row could develop, Peter and Andrew had pounded breathlessly down the last few steps.

'Come on, you lot, there's no time for arguing now. Look, he's coming back again,' Peter yelled. 'We must find that path quickly.'

Fire continued to pour from the doorway of the wizards' lair and by its light they made out a dark hole through the undergrowth just to their left.

'This must be it,' cried Andrew. 'Come on.'

They scrambled through to find themselves in a low tunnel cut through dense holly bushes.

'Whew. Well, we should be safe in here,' puffed Fumble.

They looked back and could make out a monstrous bird flapping outside and screeching in fury. Its sour stench assailed their nostrils.

'Let's not hang about,' said Peter. 'This is too close for comfort.' He hesitated. 'I do hope Sarah's all right. I suppose that bird was telling the truth?'

'Well, we can't do anything about it now, can we?' his brother replied. 'But I think he's OK. After all, Gilmere seemed to make him glow. I think he must be on our side.'

Peter nodded. 'Well, come on then. Let's find that boat. I wonder how far away it is.'

*   *   *

Sarah had never experienced anything like it in all her

life – the feeling of immense power as Arca's tremendous wing-thrusts lifted them upwards; the rushing sound of the wind past her ears, tearing at her clothes; the dizzy view of the forest below as they whirled into the twilight sky. It was breathtaking and scary too. She clutched tightly at the eagle's neck.

Suddenly, Arca let out a wild screech of primeval fierceness. The three Grims had come to do battle with them and now circled menacingly – shadowy vultures of death outlined against the pale afterglow of early evening. One swooped in close, fangs snapping and talons outstretched, seeking to tear Sarah from her feathery perch. She screamed; but Arca was quick and strong and easily outmanoeuvred his enemy. The other Grims tried the same attack with equal lack of success.

Sarah's confidence grew. The eagle's back felt warm and secure and the thrill of battle began to stir in her. She remembered then that Peter had given her Gilmere and, gripping tight with her knees, she took it from her jacket pocket.

'Enough of this,' cawed Arca. He whirled upwards in a steep climb, then turned in mid-flight and plummeted like a stone towards his enemy below. Sarah clung to his neck and flipped open the lid of Gilmere. Light streamed forth as intense as a laser beam and before Arca's claws could strike, the Grim beneath them shrivelled to a cinder and vanished in a puff of smoke. Arca blinked.

'You deny me my prey, Sarah Brown, but I do not begrudge it you, for they are merciless creatures who would kill you if they could.'

The two remaining Grims closed in fast, one from above and one from below. Arca streaked across the sky as they homed in on their target and Sarah gritted her teeth for the moment of impact. Then, with astonishing skill and enormous strength, Arca threw open his wings and stopped in mid-flight. The move was too much for the Grims and they hurtled headlong into one another, colliding with a mighty crash. One dropped like a stone into the trees far below, mortally wounded. The other, sensing defeat, quickly recovered, turned, and flew hard and low back towards the sanctuary of Hagbane's castle.

'We shall not let this one escape,' cried Arca as he set off in rapid pursuit. 'Death to the enemies of Elmesh!'

Although fear propelled the Grim at great speed, the eagle was faster and the gap closed rapidly. Sarah opened the mirror and tried to focus the beam on the foe but could not do so. It looked as if he would gain the castle. Indeed, they were right over the ramparts when Arca struck. His talons sank deep into the Grim's neck. With a horrifying screech the creature writhed and fought to shake off its attacker. Sarah clung on in desperation as the giants fought. Then Arca executed a deathblow with his sharp beak and the Grim fell mangled to the courtyard beneath.

At once, Arca began to climb, but hardly a moment too soon, for a crackle of fire leapt from the wand of a furious Hagbane who had followed the action from her castle ramparts. She screamed with rage as the fiery bolt merely singed the tail feathers of the victor. Sarah saw the Shadow-witch's face contorted in hatred, her clenched fists shaking in anger as they made their escape.

'Whew, that was close,' she gasped.

'Yes, but we are safe now,' the eagle replied as he climbed away into the night. 'Now I must take you to a place of rest and refreshment so that you may renew your strength.'

The excitement over, Sarah suddenly felt very weak and sick. She closed her eyes and, nestling against the eagle's back, sank into oblivion.

*   *   *

Peter and Andrew and the three mice had struggled along the secret path in pitch darkness. It turned out to be an extremely muddy and tortuous route through a tangle of holly, hawthorn and gorse bushes, and the two boys had to scramble bent double most of the time. The further downhill the path plunged the muddier it grew, until they were slithering and sliding through the clawing prickles. When they eventually emerged by the riverside, they were exhausted and miserable, and covered in mud and scratches.

'Yeuk, I thought that would never end!' exclaimed Andrew. 'I wonder where we are now.'

'Anywhere's better than back there,' Peter replied. 'I hope Sarah's all right, that's all. I wonder when we'll see her again – and Arca, too, for that matter.'

'It's a good job he came when he did. I wouldn't have fancied our chances against those black bat things,' said Andrew. 'I'm sure Arca has saved Sarah. He didn't look as though he needed anyone to look after him, did he?'

'Hm, I wonder where those two rotten wizards have gone.'

'Well, not back to their lair, that's for sure. You certainly put an end to that,' laughed Andrew.

'We were stupid to be taken in by them. Just think what might have happened to us!' Peter shivered at the thought.

A call from Grumble interrupted their conversation. 'Hey, we think we've found the boat. Over here.'

They followed the direction of his voice until Andrew tripped over Fumble and fell on the muddy ground with a loud *splat*.

'Ouch, who was that? As if I couldn't guess. Where are you?'

'Over here.'

In the darkness they could just make out the shape of a small rowing boat hauled up on the bank. They crowded round it.

'Do you know where we are?' Peter asked.

'We know this river. It's the Wendle,' answered Fumble. 'It should be possible to get back to Trotter but at night time everything looks so different. I'm not sure I'll recognise when to stop.'

'We can't afford to make a mistake because it goes fairly close to Hagbane's castle,' added Grumble. 'I for one don't want to go back there.'

'Nor me,' said Peter with feeling. 'That settles it then; wizards or no wizards, Grims or no Grims, we're staying here tonight. I'm too tired to go on, anyway. Does anyone think different?'

Nobody did and so the three mice and the two boys clambered into the boat, which fortunately was dry, and snuggled up together for warmth as best they could. Before long, the drama and exhaustion of the day overtook them and they all fell fast asleep. Nothing stirred as they slept, and the dark river flowed silently beneath the cold light of the moon and stars.

8

The Fairy Queen

In front of Prince Oswain stretched the bleak moor known as the Waste Plains; behind lay the inhospitable mountains of Cadaelin, their peaks already shrouded in cloud as if to bar his way back should he try. Farther ahead eastwards, out of sight across the rolling moor with its scrubby grass and heather, lay the Great Forest of Alamore and the reason for his journey.

The keen wind and dull sky matched his mood as he tramped through the long hours. The days to come would test him; and though he hoped to win through, he could not be certain. Oswain suspected that the battles would be fierce but as yet he had little inkling of what kind they might be. Strong and well trained though he was, he would have to muster all his courage, wisdom and skill in readiness for the challenge when it came.

In such a sombre frame of mind he marched the day through until, at length, he came to within sight of the Great Forest itself. A dark expanse of wintry trees stretched from one end of the horizon to the other, and before it in the fading light of evening glinted the serpentine silver thread of the River Wendle.

'Tomorrow, I shall enter the forest and see what shall befall me,' he breathed. Somewhere in the distance he heard the wild screeching of birds.

* * *

A cold, pale dawn awoke the company in the boat; the trees stood stark and grey in the mist that lay over the river.

'Brr, it's cold,' shivered Andrew, his teeth chattering as he arose.

'Oof! Ouch! Oh, my leg, it's stuck,' Peter grunted. 'Ugh, I do feel stiff. Ouch!'

Slowly and lazily the three mice uncurled themselves from where they had huddled together.

'Reckon they slept better than us,' Andrew laughed ruefully. 'Ow, my neck doesn't half hurt. I wonder what time it is.'

'No idea, but we'd better get back to Trotter as soon as possible. They'll be worried sick about us. Come on, you mice, wakey wakey!'

'Go away,' groaned Grumble. 'Give us some peace and quiet.'

'Grummffn,' added Mumble.

'Breakfast time,' Andrew called – and in an instant all three mice were awake. 'Egg, chips, baked beans and bacon.'

'Oh, shut up! You're only making me feel even hungrier,' Peter complained. 'Come on, everyone. If we want breakfast we'll have to get a move on or there will be none left. Plenty of water, though!' he added, nodding towards the river.

'I wonder what sort of night Sarah's had. She's probably tucking into eggs and bacon at the Trotters' right now. Lucky thing!'

'Well, let's hope we soon join her,' Peter answered. 'Anyway, keep an eye open for those two wizards. I don't think we've seen the last of them, somehow. How on earth did we let them take us in like that? We must be stupid. I felt something was wrong the moment we met them, you know, but I didn't take any notice of it.'

'Perhaps that's the trouble; none of us did,' said his brother. 'Anyway, the quicker we get moving, the farther away we'll be from them. Come on, let's get this boat into the water.'

'Wait for us, then. We don't want to be left behind,' said Grumble, who felt cheated out of his breakfast.

So the boys and the mice together heaved and shoved until the boat slid with a slight splash into the water.

'Look out! Hold on to her or she'll float away,' cried Andrew. 'Grab that rope, quick!'

He pointed to a rope trailing from the prow. Fumble, who was nearest, leapt for it and caught the end. Unfortunately, he caught his feet as well and found himself being dragged along the bank in a complete tangle as the boat drifted downstream.

'Ow! Help! Ouch!' he cried.

The others chased after him and just managed to prevent him being dragged into the water.

'Stupid clot!' exclaimed Grumble. 'That nearly cost us the boat. Then where would we have been?'

'Walking, I suppose,' retorted Fumble. 'Oh, my head hurts!'

'Don't you . . .'

'Hey,' laughed Peter. 'Come on, you two. We've got the boat, so it's all right. Hop in now and let's be on our way.'

Everyone clambered aboard and Peter pushed away

from the bank with a broken branch. Soon they were drifting along in a pleasant light current. The sun rose above the trees and the air felt surprisingly warm, almost like spring. For a little while, they could forget their worries and cares and could bask in the sunshine while the water lapped and gurgled around the boat and the banks slid by. Andrew leaned back and trailed his fingers in the water, pretending that they were miniature water-skiers racing each other to the breakfast table.

For most of their journey the trees came right down to the water's edge but every so often a small grassy clearing broke the monotony. Fumble told them that one of these clearings had a landmark, a small boulder, indicating the path to Trotter's house. So they took it in turns to watch out for it.

'Loo, prittyflors.'

Mumble tugged at Peter's sleeve. He was pointing to a clearing ahead of them on the left bank. Peter heaved himself up from the bottom of the boat where he had been lying and everyone crowded to see what Mumble was pointing at. Nobody, of course, had understood what he had said.

'Look at that!' cried Peter. 'Those are flowers, I'm sure.'

'We've not had flowers in the forest for years,' said Fumble. 'How unusual. We should stop and look. I wonder what it means.'

The flowers made a patch of bright yellow that glowed like new gold in the morning sun, contrasting sharply with the drabness all around. But as they drew closer it became apparent that the flowers were not flowers at all but something even more amazing.

'They're alive,' exclaimed Peter in wonder. 'They're

moving. I don't believe it but I think they're . . . they look like fairies!'

Now Peter had never seen fairies before in his life, but sure enough, there were dozens of little yellow figures prancing about on the grass in the sunshine, and he could think of no other way to describe them. The light glistened off their gossamer wings and happy laughter accompanied their dancing. As they drew closer, a sweet, heady scent wafted over the entranced onlookers and they worked out that it came from large yellow puffballs that the fairies were tossing one to the other. Every so often one would burst in a shower of scented pollen dust that drifted over the water, carried towards them by a light breeze.

Peter pushed the tiller over until the boat ran lightly aground on the bank side. As soon as they came to rest, a fairy, who was taller and of greater splendour than the rest, emerged from the dance. She wore a magnificent daffodil-yellow robe edged with gold and a golden crown adorned her long blonde tresses. Smiling, she approached them with grace and poise in every movement.

'It must be the queen of the fairies, or something,' whispered Andrew.

'Hail, travellers,' she cried in a sweet, musical voice. 'Welcome to you on this fine morning!'

'Er, um, hello,' stammered Peter, unsure of how you addressed a fairy queen. 'Er, excuse me, but you . . . you are fairies, aren't you?'

The queen replied with a laugh. 'Why, yes, indeed we are. And I am their queen. And yourselves? Pray tell me, who are you?'

'Well, we're travellers, actually, though we're not

going very far. We're looking for the path that will lead us to Trotter the badger. Do you know where it is?'

'Why, yes, of course. It's around the next two bends in the river. But what brings you this way in the first place, dare I ask?'

Andrew spoke. 'If you please, ma'am, we've just escaped from two wizards and a great eagle rescued our sister. That was last night. So we're trying to meet up again.'

'Then you have not eaten?' the queen enquired.

'No, not a thing, your highness,' replied Grumble, who could feel his stomach grumbling.

The queen clapped her hands. At once, two fairies came forward bearing a golden goblet filled with a clear liquid.

'Drink this,' she invited. 'It is a magic nectar that will refresh you and give you strength for the rest of your journey.'

Peter remembered his mistake of the night before and hesitated. Seeing this, the queen smiled.

'Ah, you think it may be poisoned, do you? I assure you, by Elmesh himself, it is not. See for yourself.'

So saying she took a long drink. Grumble agreed to have a sip and, to their relief, pronounced it very good. So they all drank of the liquid, which turned out to be utterly delicious and at once, as the fairy queen had promised, they felt much better. The events of the day before and the uncomfortable night in the boat all began to fade like a nasty dream. Peter pushed the boat back into the water and, waving cheerfully to the fairies, he jumped in as once more it began to drift down the river.

'Farewell, brave travellers,' called the queen after them

as she waved goodbye. 'On your way.'

'Bye, bye, dear fairies. Thank you,' sighed Peter, who now felt warm and relaxed. He flopped down in the boat and closed his eyes. 'Keep an eye open for the second bend, won't you?' he said to nobody in particular.

Fumble had never felt so confident before; he walked all the way around the gunwale of the boat without falling once and finished up balancing on the prow on one paw.

Mumble addressed the crew with perfect diction: 'My dear fellow-mice, yeomen among the forest-folk, and Peter, and Andrew, Children of Time Beyond Time and fair visitors to our realm. What a grand company is gathered here! The wizards are defeated, the Grims too. Soon wicked Hagbane herself will fall. Nothing will stop us, gentlemen.'

He sat down to applause from everyone, especially Grumble who clapped and cheered and finally burst out laughing. The effect was contagious and soon all five lay doubled up in the bottom of the boat, hooting with laughter until their sides ached. Which is why none of them looked back.

If they had, the sight would have sobered them up in an instant. Where the bright fairies had danced, there remained nothing but a black, stinking patch of rotting weeds and the fairy queen was no more than a bent slimy stalk.

The whole thing had been a clever delusion created by Hagbane herself. Back in her castle she gloated over her crystal ball in which she had seen and controlled everything.

'Meddling brats! It worked even better than I expected.

I shall destroy them now, once and for all. Heh, heh, heh!'

Her laughter continued and the sun passed behind the clouds. Still quite intoxicated by the magic nectar, the company in the boat failed to notice that the river was beginning to flow faster and more turbulently. They also missed the landmark that indicated the path back to Trotter's house. The little boat began to bob and buck in the current and soon it was racing along while the crew were quite unaware that matters were fast getting out of control.

Having rounded the two bends the boat began to hurtle along a straight stretch of river strewn with boulders. The muted roar of a steep waterfall grew louder and louder. Bobbing like a cork and trapped in the surging current the boat hurtled along, while its occupants lay laughing helplessly with no idea of the danger they faced.

Suddenly, there was a sickening crunch as the boat crashed into one of the jagged rocks that jutted from the river bed. Water poured over the bows, dowsing everyone on board, while the current hurled the boat forward once again.

The effect of this sudden cold soaking was to bring the mice and the boys to their senses. Peter scrambled up and peered over the gunwale. He gasped with fright as he saw the menacing rapids through which they were rushing, and the apparent end of the river right ahead of them.

'Quick, everyone,' he yelled. 'We're heading straight for a waterfall!'

The boat crashed and ricocheted off the rocks one more time and then shot towards the brink.

The crew covered their faces, expecting the worst, when with a bone-jarring crash their craft slammed into more rocks and jammed fast between two boulders right on the very edge of the falls.

The force of the impact was so great that Fumble was thrown overboard and would have been swept to his death if his leg had not once more caught in the rope. Gurgling and spluttering, choking in the foam and spray, he struggled to stay alive in the swirling current. Quickly Peter grabbed the rope and hauled the poor mouse back on board, dripping and very sorry for himself.

The boat creaked and groaned beneath them and began rapidly to fill with water. It was quite obvious that it would soon break up and that, unless help came, they were lost. The hissing roar of the waterfall drowned out all possibility of speech so Peter made signs to say that they could do nothing except shout together for all they were worth.

'Help! Help!' they cried. 'Somebody please help us!'

9

Safe and Sound

The warmth of the morning sun woke Sarah from an untroubled sleep. Lazily, she opened her eyes and squinted against the sun's glare. She gave a dreamy smile and her hand felt the softness of the sheepskin rug on which she lay. For a long moment she imagined she was in her own bedroom back home.

Then it all began to come back to her – the flight from Hagbane's castle, the awful wizards, how she had felt when Arca swooped towards her, that tremendous battle against the Grims – and then, her mind was a blank. She didn't know what had taken place after that. Where was she? She sat up with a jolt and gazed around her. To her astonishment she was lying near the entrance of a small, sunlit cave high up on a rocky precipice. A breathtaking view of Alamore stretched before her – an immense ocean of treetops, with silvery rivers and purple mountains in the hazy distance. The air smelt fresh and invigorating and she breathed deeply. 'Arca must have brought me here,' she thought to herself. 'I wonder where he's got to.'

She got up and made her way to the cave entrance. The sight made her gasp, for below her the rock fell sheer away to a dizzy depth beyond her imaginings. She stepped back quickly, realising that she was very high up a mountain and only Arca could remove her. As she looked around the cave, she noticed for the first time a bowl of clear liquid and a lump of bread. It reminded her that she had not eaten or drunk for a long time so she quickly tucked in, thankful to Arca for his thoughtfulness. The liquid tasted sweet and tangy and, whatever it was, it made her feel full of life and energy. She flopped back upon her sunlit bed to wait for Arca's return. The air about her seemed wonderfully good and clean and for the first time since she and her brothers had arrived in Caris Meriac she felt not a care in the world. She decided to call the drink 'Arca-ade'.

*   *   *

Far, far below and on the opposite side of the Great Forest, Prince Oswain came to the banks of the River Wendle. There he found the ford and crossed from the Waste Plains into the shadows of the tall barren trees. No one noticed his arrival except the trees, some of which seemed to tremble at his coming as though they were expecting him.

'My journey is almost ended and my destiny about to begin,' he announced to the silent woods. So saying, he plunged into the depths of the Forest.

*   *   *

'Help! Somebody rescue us,' cried Peter. 'Help!'
The water continued to crash about them and another

piece of the boat snapped off with a sharp splintering noise and was carried over the roaring falls to the rocks below. By now, what with the spray and the water that more than half-filled their disintegrating boat, the boys and the mice were soaked to the skin. Andrew wondered how much longer they could last out, for already he was growing numb with cold and his teeth were chattering. Peter reckoned the boat had only minutes to survive before the force of the water smashed it to matchwood. He called out even more earnestly.

Then, just as they were beginning to lose hope, a faint voice called from the bank.

'Hold on. We'll soon have you out of there. Don't worry. Just hold on.'

'It's Trotter!' Andrew shouted. 'Hooray! And look, there's Stiggle and lots of other animals with him.'

A large company of the forest-folk was waving to them from the riverside. They all waved back in desperation.

'But how are they going to rescue us?' bellowed Peter above the roar of the falls.

'I don't know, but Trotter seems pretty sure he can do it,' his brother replied. 'Look, he's sorting out something or other.'

The next moment, they saw a fluttering of black wings, and to their surprise several blackbirds began to fly across the intervening water. Dangling from their claws was a length of rope.

Peter laughed. 'Fantastic! Look at that. It's a lifeline.'

The rescue was a marvellous piece of teamwork. The blackbirds dropped their line into the eager hands of the boat crew and Trotter called out instructions from the bank. They might have hauled the mice across together but nobody wanted to risk being with Fumble in case he messed it up, and Grumble refused to go with Mumble in case they didn't understand one another properly! So the crowd on the bank heaved away at the rope and dragged the mice across one by one. Well-wishers surrounded each soggy heap of fur that was brought to safety, and there was much cheering as the blackbirds flew off with the rope for the next one.

'Our turn now,' Peter shouted. 'You go next, Andrew. No, don't argue; we haven't much time before this thing breaks up. Go on!'

After the briefest hesitation, Andrew plunged into the icy current, the chill taking his breath away. For one awful moment it looked as if the forest-folk wouldn't have the strength to pull him out and he would be swept over the top. However, they never lost their determination and after a lot of heaving and blowing they managed to pull him safely to the shore.

'Get the rope to Peter. Quick!' he gasped.

They were only just in time; with a final sickening crunch, the boat broke into pieces and disappeared over the falls. Peter clutched in desperation at the rock and only just managed to grab hold of the rope. His journey through the raging torrent was a little easier than Andrew's because Andrew was able to pull the rope as well, but it was still hard work and everyone was much relieved when he finally climbed out of the water to rejoin his friends.

'Thank you, thank you, Trotter,' Peter panted. 'And everyone. Thank you ever so much. You turned up just in time.'

'But how did you know?' Andrew asked. 'Did you

hear us calling?'

'All in good time,' replied Trotter with a smile. 'The first thing to do is to get you home and dry with something to eat. You have done very well, all of you. I feel extremely proud of you. But we must go. No more questions until we've had some of Mrs T's cooking, eh, Andrew?'

So it was that three-quarters of an hour later they were gathered around a blazing fire in Trotter's home, drinking tea following a splendid meal. The boys and the mice were feeling much better and had more or less dried out.

'Now then, Trotter, please tell us what's been happening and how you found us,' said Peter.

'Very well,' replied the old badger. 'Aldred and I waited for a long time after you went into the castle but nothing happened. We began to fear the worst and think you had fallen into a trap. Then we saw Hagbane in her tower conjuring up that snowstorm. We knew then that you must have been successful and so tried to find you, but the storm was too bad. We searched for hours until it was quite dark but even our best trackers could find no trace of you, what with the snow covering the ground around her castle.'

'That's because we were underground by then,' interrupted Andrew. He went on to tell them of Terras and Sorda and of their escape.

'Ah, that's how it happened, is it? No wonder we couldn't find you.'

'Did you know of those wizards?' asked Peter.

'Rumours have reached us of some mischief afoot.' It was Aldred who spoke. 'Forest-folk have been disappearing without trace and those Grims have been seen flying at dusk, but we hadn't realised the connection until now. It's utterly awful.'

'I agree,' added Stiggle. 'If I ever get my claws on those two. . . .'

'Well, to continue,' Trotter interrupted. 'We kept searching, hoping to find a clue and then the great eagle, Arca, came. He told us what had happened and advised us to get some rest. He returned this morning to help us in the search. The eye of one such as Arca misses little and he directed us to the waterfall. He had seen what happened to you.'

'I still don't quite understand what really did happen on the river,' said Andrew. 'All I know is, we met some fairies and the next thing I remember is the waterfall.'

'That is not too difficult to explain,' Trotter answered. 'You were the victims of one of Hagbane's tricks. There are no fairies in the forest but she created a delusion that fooled you and took away your control of the boat. As far as she is concerned it was as good a way as any to destroy you.'

'And she very nearly did,' said Peter. 'What an idiot I was to be taken in twice.'

'You weren't the only one,' his brother consoled him. 'We were all tricked this time. Just thank goodness for Arca's help.'

'Evil has often copied good,' said Trotter seriously. 'Do not trust to appearances or words, particularly smooth and flattering words. Remember too, Peter, that a thing of great evil can also be a thing of beauty; nor are ugly things necessarily bad. You must learn to see the inner-ness of things and especially of people, if you want to be wise.'

Peter wasn't sure that he understood, so Aldred tried

to explain. 'Arca is a good example of what Trotter means. He frightens me, to tell you the truth, and he's a strange creature, living in a high and lonely world, where he holds his own counsels. But he's altogether good and he is a messenger of Elmesh. He'll return to us soon – and with Sarah. Oh, she's all right, you know. Perfectly safe with Arca, she is, even if he does scare me.'

Peter and Andrew were delighted to know that their sister was safe and were thrilled to have a report of the aerial battle against the Grims and the part she had played in it.

'I wish we'd stayed behind to watch,' said Andrew.

'No you don't,' Peter answered. 'Just remember that Grim!'

As they talked, the mice grew drowsy in front of the fire and soon fell fast asleep, curled up on top of one another.

'They were marvellous,' laughed Peter, looking at them. 'You were right, Stiggle. They were the ideal choice.'

Stiggle smiled towards Aldred, who grudgingly agreed. Trotter suddenly became serious again.

'Listen,' he said. 'All this worries me. I do not pretend to know all that Elmesh is doing. Doubtless he has good reason for sending you children here, but it is obvious to me that even with Gilmere you are no match for Hagbane.'

'I agree,' said Peter. 'Can I be honest? Ever since we arrived here I've felt completely out of my depth. I mean, it's really no use asking kids like us to help you fight Hagbane. Then there's Terras and Sorda as well. I don't even know where to start.'

'We do have Arca on our side,' his brother reminded him.

Peter shrugged.

'He is quite a fighter,' said Aldred. 'But I'm not sure if even he could beat Hagbane single-handed. Trouble is, so many of our best troops are locked up in her castle. If only we could rescue them things would be easier.'

'I know,' said Peter. 'I saw some of them. They looked pretty well beyond hope. I'm only sorry that we couldn't rescue any. There must be a way to get them out.'

'We need help,' Trotter declared. 'I don't know where it is to come from, but I shall enquire of Elmesh tonight. I cannot risk your lives again. Things are too unevenly matched at present and until matters change I think we must simply lie low and keep out of harm's way as best we can. Though, goodness knows, she will be out hunting us soon enough.'

They sat brooding over the problem. Nobody really knew what to say and the longer they sat the more oppressive the enemy seemed. A dark despair settled over their spirits like a low winter cloud.

Suddenly there were noises outside; a heavy footstep, a cracking twig. Everyone jumped as the sounds broke their silence.

Then, slowly, with a light creak of the hinges the door swung open, and a long black shadow fell across the floor. Horrified, Mrs Trotter screamed aloud and dropped her teacup with a crash.

10

Oswain Takes Charge

Fear and dismay paralysed everyone in the room as they stared at the long shadow that darkened the threshold. Surely Hagbane had come in person to wreak her vengeance! Not an eye blinked as the shadow advanced.

Yet it was no evil-looking Hagbane who entered the room a moment later. Instead, they found themselves confronted by a tall stranger dressed in a hooded, green travelling cloak, the cowl of which completely hid his face. For a moment, nobody moved; then Aldred whipped out his sword and leapt forward. All his doubts about the children came flooding back. If this wasn't Hagbane, then he could only be one of the wizards or some other enemy.

'Show yourself,' growled the stoat, 'before I run you through.'

The stranger laughed and threw back his cowl. A clean-shaven young man of handsome features stood before them, noble yet kindly in his bearing, and with dark eyes that flashed with an inner fire.

'There will be no need for that, Aldred.' His voice was rich and deep. 'Allow me to introduce myself. I am Prince Oswain, the son of Argil, High King of Elmar, and of all lands Westwards. My mother is Queen Talesanna.'

He smiled and bowed slightly. There was an authority in his manner, and a fearlessness, that made Aldred lower his sword. The stranger looked about him.

'You must be Peter and you, Andrew – the Brown children. Yes, and you are Trotter, the noble lore-master of the forest-folk, if I am not mistaken. To you, I offer my apologies for having entered your house unannounced, but I felt such discretion was wise.'

He turned to Mrs Trotter. 'My special apologies to you, dear lady of the house, for causing you such fright. Please forgive me.'

'Well, I'm sure I do, sir,' replied a flustered Mrs Trotter.

'That's fine and well,' Aldred spoke again. 'But shouldn't you explain yourself a bit more? Like, for instance, who sent you? Whose side are you on? Why are you here? And how come you know so much about us?'

The tall stranger smiled. 'Of course. You are quite right and I will do so; but first, may I put you all at ease by saying that I have come to the Great Forest of Alamore at the bidding of Elmesh himself.'

'If that is so, you are truly welcome,' said Trotter. 'But you will understand our caution when I tell you that our enemy is a skilled mistress of deception and we have had much sore experience of that in recent times. To say you are from Elmesh is a strong statement, my friend. What proof do you bring?'

Oswain glanced at them each in turn. 'I give you first my oath that it is so and I do so by the fire of the Merestone and by the light of Elrilion. But, for your eyes, I have this to show you in token of my word.'

He removed his glove and showed them a ring upon the second finger of his right hand. The ring was large and of intricately fashioned gold, but what caught everyone's attention was the jewel set within it. This was no ordinary diamond or emerald; it did not catch light and reflect it. This jewel smouldered and flashed with its own fire like no other that any had ever seen. Trotter inspected it closely, gazing in awe and wonder.

'Yes, you judge correctly,' said the stranger, without waiting for Trotter to speak. 'It is of the same kind as the Merestone, for it is a fragment of that jewel itself.'

'Sit down, please,' whispered the old badger. 'I need no further proof. For one who has gazed upon the Merestone, it is enough. It is enough.'

The badger ushered Oswain to the best seat in the room, and everyone, even Aldred, relaxed.

Once they were all seated Oswain began to answer their questions.

'Several years ago I was given this ring by my mother, Queen Talesanna. She would not say how she came by it but I remember feeling that it had cost her much suffering to obtain it. It has never been removed from my hand and nor could it be now, as you can see. Yet it is to be removed, for it is spoken that this jewel shall again be reunited with the Merestone, the manner of which I do not yet know.'

'The prophecy,' interrupted Peter looking eagerly at Trotter. 'The one you showed us.'

'Yes,' Trotter nodded. 'It is so. Then you, Oswain, are the promised ruler, the coming one who shall set the Great Forest free. I was not mistaken concerning the signs, nor with regard to the children. Elmesh be praised! Sire, I am your servant and at your command.'

He bowed low before Prince Oswain and the others followed suit.

'I'll put the kettle on,' said Mrs Trotter. 'It's not every day we have royalty in our home.'

Oswain smiled at her. 'If you but knew it, Mrs Trotter, you are of royal blood yourselves, for true nobility comes not by birth but by how one handles pain and adversity.'

Mrs Trotter's fur bristled with embarrassment and she hurried out to make the tea.

'Are you aware, sir, of the whereabouts of the Merestone at this time and of the dreadful plight that is ours?' asked Stiggle.

'I know of it and my destiny involves its recovery, and the destruction of the dark force that oppresses you. That is why I am here and, though I fear it will be a hard battle, it will be won. Do not doubt that.'

'Did Elmesh tell you all our names too?' queried Andrew.

Oswain laughed. 'No. There is a very simple answer to that question. I have spoken with Arca already. He has told me much.'

'Arca! Of course. And Sarah. Is Sarah all right?'

'She is very well, as you will see for yourselves quite soon. We have already met briefly. So come now, and let us meet properly.'

So saying, he led the company outside and, gazing up into the sky, uttered a long shrill whistle. For a moment nothing happened and then they spied a small dot high among the clouds. It grew rapidly as Arca plummeted to the earth. Great wings outspread, he landed a few metres away from where they stood. And there was Sarah, with her hair flying all over the place, clutching at his neck.

'Sarah!'

'Oh Peter, Andrew, thank goodness you're safe. Oh, I'm so glad to see you again!'

She slipped from Arca's back and threw her arms

around her brothers. For a while they had no words to express what they felt but after that there was no stopping them.

'I've been to the most wonderful place, a cave in the mountains. The view was fantastic.'

'What's it like riding on Arca's back?'

'Did you really kill a Grim yourself?'

'Isn't Oswain brilliant? Arca and I met him earlier this afternoon. What do you think he's going to do?'

At that moment Mrs Trotter came to the door with a tray of steaming mugs.

'What a to-do,' she exclaimed. 'I come into the front room and you've all gone. And there I am standing here with all these cups of tea to drink. Sarah! You're back, my dear. Here, somebody take these while I give her a kiss.'

Peter went across to Arca.

'Um, I want to say thank you for saving Sarah's life and, well, all of us really. You've been brilliant.'

'Elmesh has sent me to play my part in the destruction of evil. He has sent you too. It was right that we met. I was glad to be in time,' croaked the eagle in reply.

'Yes, well, thank you anyway,' Peter replied.

'You must not mind Arca's ways,' said Oswain joining them. 'He is one who inhabits harsh and lonely places. He does not feel as we do, except to do the will of Elmesh. That is his one satisfaction. Now I must speak with him out here for a little while, since he will not enter the confines of a house, and we have to make plans before nightfall. So please excuse us.'

* * *

The rest of that afternoon was spent discussing how they might defeat Hagbane. Everyone felt more confident and determined now that Oswain was with them. He was the sort of person who made you feel that you mattered and that together you could win the game. No one questioned his right to leadership in the campaign, and he largely directed their discussions.

'We need to be wise,' he said. 'It would be no victory if Hagbane escaped with the Merestone. We must recapture that at all costs.'

This rather put paid to Andrew's suggestion that they should simply blow her up in her castle, assuming that they possessed explosives – which they didn't. They needed a more subtle plan.

Aldred spoke up. 'It seems to me that we must rescue the prisoners before we do anything else. Some of my finest troops are in her dungeons and she will certainly kill them if she so much as suspects an attack. In fact, I should think they're at great risk even now after recent events.'

'Yes, and she can always blackmail us while she has them. Their lives for her terms,' added Stiggle.

'I agree,' answered Oswain. 'Then that must be our first priority.' His eyes scanned the group. 'Now, we need to find a way of drawing her and her guards away from the castle. We must find her weak spot. Any ideas?'

'Oh, that's easy enough,' said Trotter. 'She is vain. The most self-conceited creature you could ever imagine.'

'She might be vulnerable to a bit of flattery then. Hmmm.'

'In that case, I think I have a plan.' It was Stiggle who spoke. Carefully, he explained to them his ideas.

'It might work. It might just work!' cried Oswain. 'Yes, let's give it a go!'

* * *

That night saw much unaccustomed activity on the part of the forest-folk. Animals scurried to and fro in the darkness and there was much whispering of instructions and passing on of progress reports. The younger animals found it especially exciting to be part of such a secret plan.

It was not until the cold dark hour before the dawn that most fell, tired but satisfied, into their beds. Indeed, if it had not been for sheer exhaustion many would have stayed awake with excitement. However, they needed their rest in order to be completely alert for the events to come.

Stage two of Stiggle's plan began quite early next morning when Fumble, Mumble and Grumble – who to the relief of many had been excused the night's work – set off once more in the direction of Hagbane's castle. Only this time they made no attempt to conceal their coming.

'Ouch, that hurt my toe,' groaned Fumble as he picked himself up after tripping on a tree root.

'Huh, if you carry on at this rate we'll never even reach the castle,' Grumble complained. 'Not that I think that would be a bad thing, if you ask me. Why does it always have to be us who get landed with the dangerous jobs, that's what I want to know? I mean, just as likely she'll kill us on the spot after the trouble we've caused her.'

'Ohstopmoanin.'

'What's that you say, Mumble? Eh? Speak up then.' Grumble was feeling very moody indeed.

'Leave him alone,' said Fumble. 'I'm sure it'll be all right anyway, if Oswain thinks so.'

'I just hope you're right, that's all I can say.'

At last they came in sight of the castle. With hearts thumping, they began to walk in full view towards the dark and forbidding main door. Dead bats hung from trees on either side of them, the sight of which made the mice shiver with disgust. Then, just as they came under the castle's shadow, a Grog guard stepped out to bar their way with his spear.

'Halt! What's yer business 'ere? Don't yer know yer trespassin'? Yer can git yer froat cut fer that.' He grinned wickedly, showing his broken yellow teeth, and brandished his spear in their faces.

'Please, sir, your honour,' began Fumble. 'We have come to beg an audience with the great Queen Hagbane. We bring an important message for her and we come in peace.'

At this point Grumble produced a white flag, and waved it before the guard.

'News, eh? And yer want ter see 'er majesty do yer? Wait 'ere, an' I'll go an' ask 'er if she wants ter see yer. An' if she don't, I'll slit yer froats,' he added as an afterthought before vanishing inside.

'Do you think it's going to work?' whispered Grumble.

'I hope so. Anyway, so far so good. Look out, here she comes!'

The Shadow-witch appeared before them as though she were made of wavering grey smoke. She fixed them with a baleful glare.

'You! Yes, I've seen you before, haven't I? With those meddling children, were you not? And you have thwarted me twice. Vermin,' she screamed. 'For that you shall die – and very slowly.'

The mice trembled but somehow managed to keep their nerve.

'Please, your majesty,' said Fumble. 'Before you kill us, please hear what we've come to say. We have come in peace with a message from the forest-folk.'

'Message? What message? Speak, vermin scum. Your life depends on whether I like what I hear.' She moved menacingly towards Fumble and towered over him.

'If it pleases you, your highness, mighty queen of the Great Forest, we deeply regret the fighting that has gone on between us over the years and we would dearly like to put matters to rights with you. Your dreadful power, your fearsome might, is never to be forgotten. Your majesty, the people of the forest crave an open-air audience with you to show you how they really feel about you.'

The Shadow-witch glared suspiciously at the mouse but then, as Trotter had correctly surmised, her vanity got the better of her. She interpreted the speech as praise.

'Really?' Her eyes gleamed. 'So you have seen sense at last, have you?'

'I believe we have, your majesty,' replied Fumble in a solemn tone.

'Very well, I shall grant you your request. Where shall it be?'

'If it pleases your highness, we would like you to come to the old clearing at noon today. It is an ancient place of honour, fitting for such an occasion.'

'And you will demonstrate your loyalty to me?'

'Your majesty, we will be prepared to demonstrate all we owe you.'

'Then this is how I shall want it shown. You will hand over those Children of Time Beyond Time to me. Do you understand? They do not belong to the forest and I must deal with them as I see fit. Is that clear?'

'B . . . b . . . but, your majesty . . .'

'Silence! You speak of owing me something. Very well, we shall soon see!'

'If you say so, ma'am,' said Grumble.

'I do say so, and I shall bring my guards too. So no tricks,' she threatened. 'If you fail, I shall take my vengeance upon you all. I shall show no mercy.'

'We understand, your majesty.'

'Then go, before I lose patience with you. No, wait. You!' She pointed at Fumble. 'You almost questioned my will. I shall keep you as a gesture of good faith. If you are deceiving me, then you shall be the first to die. Guard, take him!'

Before the others could protest, Fumble was marched firmly away to the dungeons, followed by Hagbane. It left Mumble and Grumble with nothing else to do except return to the others.

'Hmmmm, that didn't work out too well. Poor old Fumble. I didn't expect that,' said Grumble. 'I hope he'll be all right.'

'Ocorsewildonwori,' said Mumble.

'What? Oh, never mind. Well, all I can say is, it's *got* to work now, for Fumble's sake.' He spoke fiercely and his whiskers twitched. 'Come on, we'd better report back to the others. Goodness knows how they're going to sort all this out.'

11

Hagbane Trips Up

The old clearing, as it was known, was an open grassy area surrounded by gorse bushes, about one kilometre from Hagbane's castle. For many years the forest-folk had used it as a meeting place when they had news to announce or they needed to talk together. No meetings had taken place since Hagbane had come to power because she wouldn't allow it, and folk felt that it was too close to her castle to take the risk.

So it was with some trepidation that the forest-folk gathered in the clearing.

To tell the truth, many would have preferred not to have come and it was only the combined efforts of Trotter and Aldred that finally persuaded them. Scary though she was, most animals had a picture of Hagbane in their minds that was far worse than the truth, and it was this that helped keep her in power. As Trotter explained to Peter, evil thrives when people make too little of it, but it also thrives when they make too much of it and so lose the courage they need to break its grip. Only those who respect the power of evil and yet believe firmly in the greater power of goodness can hope to win.

Peter wasn't sure that he completely understood, but when he saw Trotter standing alone and unafraid at the head of the uneasy band of animals he knew that the badger had a special kind of courage.

A weak sun filtered through the silvery-grey sky, giving small comfort as the hour of meeting drew near. Everyone waited in silence; then Aldred called out that the Shadow-witch was on her way, together with a large company of Grogs. Each animal nervously checked his position and waited. Soon they could see the gaunt, shadowy shape striding towards them, hair and cloak swirling, and with the gang of Grogs marching raggedly behind her.

High in the sky Arca hovered between the clearing and the sun, so as not to be seen. From her perch on his back Sarah looked down on the forest. She could make out the dark specks of the animals huddled together in the grassy clearing. A little farther away she could see the castle and the paths that led from it. Hagbane and her Grogs were on their way.

'Now is our chance,' cawed Arca, who saw it all much better, of course. 'But we must hurry. There won't be much time.'

So saying, he soared in a wide sweeping arc and then swooped low over the tree tops, out of Hagbane's line of vision, and over the castle walls. Sarah braced herself and prepared to use the mirror. It was as well that she did because the remaining guards rushed them the very moment they landed. Gilmere shot forth its fearsome light, striking one Grog after another. Sarah lost count but, as before, each one turned into a frightened frog, fleeing for its life. The opposition collapsed with scarcely a croak.

'So far so good,' panted Sarah, closing the mirror. 'Now what?'

Glancing around the courtyard they saw a number of

iron-barred gates from which all sorts of animals stared wide-eyed.

'Don't be afraid,' called Sarah. 'We've come to rescue you.'

She ran from gate to gate, focusing the mirror on the locks. In an instant the doors flew open and the animals were free. Many could hardly believe it and walked out stunned; others leapt free with great joy; some who were very weak had to be carried from their cells. However, in a short time a great crowd of stoats, foxes, weasels, squirrels, moles, voles and badgers had assembled in the courtyard. Sarah, meanwhile, had run downstairs to the basement cells where Peter had been held. There she found many more animals and busied herself releasing them. It was here, too, that she found Fumble, who was so overjoyed to see her that he flung himself against her and brought them both crashing to the ground in fits of laughter.

Arca, meanwhile, organised an airlift over the walls for the weakest of the animals so that they could escape into the seclusion of the trees as soon as possible. At length, Sarah came panting up the stairs followed by a jubilant host of creatures. She ran across to the main gate and trained Gilmere's light onto the lock, muttering a prayer to Elmesh that it would work. Slowly, the great oak doors swung back, and the wide open space of freedom beckoned the prisoners.

It was then that misfortune struck. Even as the gates opened, a loud, raucous trumpet sounded from high on the castle wall.

'It must be some kind of alarm,' gasped Sarah in dismay. 'Quick, all of you, run for it! Run for your lives!'

* * *

Hagbane strode purposefully into the clearing, plainly in a no-nonsense mood. She stopped before the assembled animals, folded her arms and fixed them with an imperious gaze. Her guards halted a little distance behind.

'Well?' she demanded. 'Here I am, your queen! Do you have someone worthy who can speak?'

She deliberately overlooked Trotter who was standing there waiting. However, the old badger was not to be outdone.

'Yes, your majesty, as lore-master of the forest-folk, I will address you.' He spoke boldly and with dignity.

Hagbane frowned in annoyance. 'Very well, speak on, whatever you call yourself. I do not recognise positions *I* have not appointed but, just this once, I will listen to you. So speak, and make it good – or I'll make it bad.' She cackled to herself at her own wit.

Trotter unfurled a scroll and cleared his throat.

'Ahem. If it pleases your majesty I, Trotter, offspring of Rufus the Strong, member of the forest elders of the noble days of the Great Forest of Alamore in Caris Meriac – The Land Beyond the Far Places – I who am appointed lore-master of the forest-folk by the command of Elmesh, address you on a matter of great importance. For a long while, indeed many years, your majesty, you have held power in this forest because you possess the Merestone. Many of us have fought against you during these years and there has been much suffering for our people, many deaths, many imprisonments. The forest has grown weary and is dying. The time has come for this to end, your majesty; the days of war must cease and peace must return to the Great Forest of Alamore. Now, we would like to express some feelings of loyalty *if* we could – but first you must show your true queenliness before us, not by violence but by returning the Merestone to its rightful place and. . . .'

'What is this insolent nonsense?' Hagbane had been growing more and more irritated by Trotter's speech. Now she could contain herself no longer. 'How dare you speak to me like this, you impudent filth! Trying to tell me what to do! Me? Hagbane, the mighty queen of all this land! You bring me out for *this*? I will have no more of it.' Her voice was hard and angry, cold as steel. She spoke through gritted teeth. 'But I will have your loyalty. Bring me those children. Bring them at once before I destroy every one of you.'

Trotter had known all along that he would have little time but had hoped to delay the Shadow-witch for as long as possible. He tried to stall her.

'I am sorry my words displease you, your majesty. Please accept my . . .'

'Enough! Where are those Children of Time Beyond Time?'

'I . . . er . . . they are not actually quite here, if you see what I mean.'

'No, I do not. Bring them this instant.'

'But, your majesty . . .'

At that moment, he was interrupted by a loud trumpeting sound that echoed across the forest. It came without doubt from the direction of her castle.

'Stop!' Hagbane cried out. Her face contorted with rage and her body shook. 'I've been tricked. Tricked! Do you hear that? It's the alarm.'

She turned to her guards, her fists clenched and her brows thunderous with fury.

'Kill them! Kill every one of them. I want no mercy. Tear them limb from limb. Rip them apart!' she screamed. 'And you can start with him.'

The Shadow-witch turned and pointed at Trotter.

Only Trotter was no longer there. Nor indeed were any of the other animals. Each one had vanished as though into thin air. Hagbane looked about her, eyes popping with amazement.

'What's the meaning of this? What trickery is going on?' she spat.

Full of rage, she strode forwards – and at once fell flat on her face. Her foot had caught itself in a deep hole barely covered by grass. For a moment the Shadow-witch lay where she had fallen; then slowly she got up, and realisation dawned on her as she saw the size and depth of the hole.

'So that's how they escaped, is it?' she hissed.

'There's another one 'ere, yer 'ighness,' called a Grog. 'And another.'

'It's a plot,' the Shadow-witch screamed. She jumped up and down in a frightful rage, cursing everyone and everything she could think of. 'Why? What are they up to? I'll make the scum pay for this.'

The holes were too small for her guards to go down and so all they could do was run around searching in the gorse. It achieved nothing.

'Come here, you fools,' the Shadow-witch called. 'Back to the castle. Run! Something's up and I don't like it.'

So saying, she gathered up her skirts and ran after her

guards as fast as her legs could carry her.

Deep in the forest, Peter tried to catch his breath as he spoke. 'Phew, that was close. I thought Trotter had misjudged it for a moment.'

'Yes,' Oswain agreed. 'Yet it worked. A brilliant idea of Stiggle's, even if it was risky.'

'What was that trumpet sound?' Andrew asked.

'I suspect it is an alarm of some kind,' Oswain said. 'Let us go and see if all is well. Although I have few fears where Arca is concerned.'

What had taken place was the result of a careful plan that had begun the night before with dozens of animals, especially moles and rabbits, digging long tunnels from behind the gorse bushes into the centre of the old clearing. From these long tunnels came shorter ones, and from these, shorter ones still until the whole area was laced with a network of tunnels. They had then dug many holes to the surface, all of which were carefully covered with grass. When the animals assembled the next day, each one had stood just in front of a hole or as near as possible (some had shared one). The moment Hagbane turned to address her guards, at a signal from Trotter, they had simply stepped backwards and bolted into the ground.

Once in the tunnels, the forest-folk had scampered away just as fast as their legs could carry them, bursting from the entrances behind the gorse and making off into the shelter of the trees. It had been a most successful way of luring Hagbane and her guards from the castle and the animals had got away without a scratch.

Deep in the woods that afternoon there was a great coming together of the forest-folk, young and old alike. It was a time of deep feelings, and many tears were shed as loved ones long separated were reunited. Prisoners who had given up hope walked around in a daze, greeting old friends and acquaintances. Parents and youngsters met again, sometimes hardly recognising one another. Tales were exchanged of brave exploits, of courage in the face of suffering, and of noble deaths. Some, whose loved ones had not returned, wept openly and were comforted by others. It was a most moving occasion.

'Isn't this brilliant?' Andrew exclaimed. 'We've won a victory at last.'

'Yes,' replied Sarah, who was crying a little herself. 'Yes, it's really wonderful. I feel, well, just so happy, so full, if you know what I mean. Letting those prisoners free was the most fantastic thing I've ever done in my life. I don't know how to describe it. Just look at them.'

'Only just in time though,' Peter added.

Sarah nodded. 'Mmm. It was getting close. I nearly died when that alarm sounded. We didn't know what would happen, so we just ran. We'd hardly reached the trees when we saw the first of her guards running back. But we did it,' she ended in triumph.

'Yes, you did it, and it is a happy day for us all. Elmesh be praised!' Trotter joined them, beaming through his spectacles. 'You know, I haven't seen such rejoicing in many a year. Not since, well, I can't even remember.' He laughed, 'This is the first real victory we've had over that Shadow-witch. She's always thwarted us before – so maybe things are changing.'

'You were great, Trotter,' Peter declared. 'I thought you were so brave to face her like that.'

'Not really, Peter. I did only what was necessary.'

'And that speech,' Andrew said. 'What *were* you going to say next?'

Trotter smiled modestly. 'Yes, it was a bit of a mouthful, wasn't it? But I was trying to take as long as possible, you see. If I had continued, I would have told her how evil she was and how Elmesh was angry with her – and that she had better change. That would have made her really angry. Then we would have done our vanishing trick.'

They were joined at that moment by Aldred. 'I owe you an apology,' he said, addressing the children. 'I should have trusted you. I'm sorry.'

Everyone assured the stoat that it was all right and that they perfectly understood his caution, and that they were so glad things had turned out well, and that his troops had been rescued.

Only Oswain kept silent as he gazed at the joyful scene. Sarah, who noticed such things, caught the far away look in his eyes, a deep sadness, a longing, a feeling too great to be expressed. She wondered what it meant and decided that she must ask him.

'Hey, look everyone!'

It was Andrew who called out and folk turned to see him pointing at the ground. Quickly, those nearby gathered around him and stared at what he had found. There, growing proudly from the dark soil, was a bright mauve crocus, the first to be seen in many a long year.

'A sign of spring,' breathed Peter. 'The power of Hagbane is beginning to break.'

12

Oswain Finds Out

It was very late before most of the forest-folk went to bed
that night. Laughter and tales of brave exploits had made
it a memorable evening and, as the light faded and the
shadows grew to dusk, the story of the meeting in the old
clearing had been told and retold with so much gusto
and imagination that you could be forgiven for thinking
that Trotter had chased the Shadow-witch away single-
handed while the rest of the animals beat the Grogs to
pulp! Others spoke of Sarah and Arca with awe and
described, with many fine words, their magnificent raid
on Hagbane's castle – even though the number of Grogs
destroyed was perhaps somewhat exaggerated.

At length, all began to quieten down and the company
at Trotter's house made their weary but happy way to
bed. Sleep came surprisingly easy for Sarah and for a
long while she slept deeply. Then, once again, she began
to dream.

*She was floating like a feather caught in the warm up-
current of a summer's day. Suddenly, great bats came whirling
around her, swooping close with their leathery wings flapping
about her head. Sarah flinched, twisted and turned to avoid
them, covering her face with her hands. She called desperately
for help. Arca screeched from where he hovered high above.
Flashes of white fire shot from his eyes and frizzled the bats to
smoking cinders that dropped harmlessly to the ground. Sarah*

112

grew sleepy, drifting higher and higher in the balmy air, lazily floating towards the sky above.

Then in her dream she awoke with a start. She was in the Shadow-witch's den, where Hagbane was feeding a wild fire, cackling with glee as she did so. A bright jewel, which Sarah knew to be the Merestone, pulsed with energy. Light flashed around the room, illuminating the madness in the Shadow-witch's face. Then to her horror, Sarah saw Oswain being dragged into the fire by Hagbane. She started to run forwards to save him, but however hard she ran she could get no nearer. She shouted and screamed but nobody could hear her voice. Anguish gripped her as the flames of the fire rose higher and higher until she could see neither the Shadow-witch nor Oswain. A roaring sheet of flame reared before her; the heat and the noise were too much. Everything went black.

Sarah awoke, shivering with cold, not sure for a moment whether she was truly awake or still dreaming. She found she was lying on the floor with a blanket tangled around her arms and legs and her body bathed in sweat. For a while she lay still, trying to understand her dream.

'What's going on with me?' she said to herself under her breath. 'I never used to dream like this, not back at home.'

Thoughts of home made her wonder about this strange adventure and how they had ever got into it. What a story she would have to tell her friends at school when they got back! If they got back. She reminded herself that she had no way of knowing whether they could.

Just then, a faint click broke her thoughts. Curious, she arose and crept to the door. She opened it without a sound, and was just in time to see Oswain vanishing through the front door of the cottage. Sarah hesitated only for a moment before deciding to follow him.

It was cool outside but fear and excitement made her insensitive to the cold. Stealthily, she crept from tree to tree, always keeping a good distance behind Oswain, afraid that he might turn around and spot her. She soon realised that he was heading for the Enchanted Glade.

Since she knew the way, Sarah no longer needed to worry about keeping up and so could follow at a slower pace to make sure she wasn't seen. As a result, she arrived at the glade only a few minutes after Oswain. She saw him staring intently into the silvery pool. Its radiance lit his face with a soft glow, allowing Sarah to see lines of deep sadness etched into his features. He shook his head slowly, his mouth forming soundless words. The powerful shoulders heaved a great sigh and his whole body shook with sorrow at what he saw.

Sarah gazed in wonder as silent tears fell from his eyes into the waiting pool, seeming themselves to catch the shimmering light of Elrilion before mingling with the clear water beneath. She couldn't help herself. A wave of pity swept over her heart and, forgetting her secrecy, she ran across to him. Oswain lifted his head with a start but, before he could say anything, she threw her arms around him and looked up into his face with her own tear-filled eyes, beseeching him.

'Please, Oswain, what is it? Why are you so sad?'

'Why are you here, Sarah?' he demanded, ignoring her question. 'Did you follow me?'

'I'm sorry, but I had a terrible dream and when I woke up I heard someone leaving. I looked out of my room and saw that it was you. So I followed you. I'm really sorry if I did wrong.'

His smile was tender, and as he looked into her eyes she felt both safe and a little afraid all at once. She imagined the stars in those deep, dark eyes.

'No, you did not do wrong, Sarah. Elmesh knows, perhaps it is altogether right for you to be here tonight.' He took her hand and they sat down beside the pool. 'Now tell me about your dream.'

Sarah felt reassured and recounted all that she could remember. Oswain listened intently until she had finished.

'Alas, it is a true vision, Sarah, for something like this is indeed going to happen,' he sighed. 'Though it is little comfort to know it beforehand,' he added.

'What do you mean?' exclaimed Sarah. 'I don't want anything awful to happen to you. I don't understand all this.'

'No, I do not expect you to, for you have fallen into something far bigger than you could possibly know,' he replied. 'However, I will try to tell you a little.'

He got up and walked a short way from her before turning to speak.

'A long time ago it was written that I should journey alone to the Great Forest of Alamore to undo a great evil and restore things as they were. The wise in my own country spoke of it being the will of Elmesh, and that I would be told in some way when to begin my journey. That happened to me in a dream not many days ago – a dream similar to yours, Sarah. In my dream I saw your faces and the face of Hagbane. I knew then that the hour of my destiny drew near. It was a hard journey in which the mountain powers of Cadaelin tried to stop me, but

Elmesh gave me strength and I arrived as it was written. As you now realise, you also came to the forest to fulfil part of the prophecy – and Arca, of course.'

'So are you to rule the forest in place of Hagbane?' Sarah asked.

'That is so,' he replied solemnly. 'It is Elmesh's decree.'

'Then why are you so sad? I don't understand. After all, we've already begun to defeat her. Yet you were sad this afternoon and now you've seen something in the pool that's made you even more unhappy.'

He nodded. 'When I set out I knew that there would be suffering and pain. I did not fear that, for even though I did not understand all that was to happen, I trusted that Elmesh would keep me safe. Yet I could not see why I should be chosen for this destiny. Even the sages in my father's household were unable to tell me that.'

'Is that what you've found out tonight?' whispered Sarah.

'Yes,' he spoke with great effort. 'Tonight, the pool has spoken and told me why it is I, and I alone, who must walk this path – and I am saddened by the knowledge.'

He turned and walked away. Sarah ran after him and pulled at his sleeve.

'Oswain, why? What is it?' she pleaded. 'Please tell me!'

He hesitated and gazed into her earnest face. Almost he spoke but nothing came.

'I am sorry, Sarah,' he answered at length. 'But I cannot speak of it. It is too much for me and I must think.'

'Oh, Oswain, this is awful. Whatever must it be? And my dream. Oh . . . my dream! Does it mean you'll die?'

He was silent and Sarah felt quite helpless. She began to sob.

'No . . . no . . . please don't let it happen. There must be another way.'

He put his hands on her shoulders and spoke quietly. 'Sarah, if it is the will of Elmesh.'

'But isn't there anything we can do? Is there no other way? Oh, why does it have to be like this?' she cried.

He shook his head slowly.

'You ask questions too deep for you to understand the answers. You must await the outcome – and there may yet be some surprises. After all, you and your brothers have a part to play in all this.'

'Fat lot of use we've been,' sniffed Sarah. 'All we've done so far is get in the way.'

'That is not true,' he reassured her. 'Tonight you have done something precious. You have brought me comfort in the loneliness of my destiny. I shall not forget that. Now come, we must be back before daylight. And, please, not a word of this to anyone.'

She nodded and tucked her arm into his.

'Look, up there. See how bright Elrilion shines tonight.'

Its light was strangely comforting and Sarah felt a little better. They made their way back to Trotter's house, where they had not been missed. Sarah slept soundly for the rest of the night.

* * *

Hagbane, however, was not sleeping. She was burning with fury. Her initial discovery of the loss of her prisoners had sent her into such an intense rage that her guards scrambled out of her way and cowered in the now empty dungeons. All the rest of that day she stormed and stamped, screeching out her hatred and vowing terrible destruction upon her enemies.

Eventually she lapsed into a gloomy, brooding silence. Gradually, her troops crept out of the dungeons and went about their business, not daring to disturb her. For many hours she neither ate nor drank.

Then her mood changed. The anger returned but this time it was not an explosive rage but a cold calculating fury. Her eyes gleamed with hatred as she thought about the forest-folk.

'I shall destroy them all this time,' she muttered. 'I shall show no mercy. I've been far too soft on them. But not any longer! Every one of them shall die and I shall extend my power till I conquer the world. No one will ever make a fool of me like this again. How dare they think they can do this to me and get away with it? To me! Hagbane the mighty!'

She began to pile together strange powders and repulsive objects on her table. Swiftly, she moved to and fro, glancing from time to time at books of magic and all the while muttering threats against her foes. At last the foul mixture was complete and she placed it in an iron bowl on a tripod in the middle of the room. She pointed her wand beneath it and, in a flash, a fire began to burn, heating the contents of the bowl.

Hagbane watched as the mixture began to simmer. Her eyes glowed yellow in the firelight and dark shadows flickered about the room. Satisfied, she went to the corner and fetched the Merestone. She placed it, still covered, on a stool to the far side of the tripod and with reverence she lifted the cloth cover. The jewel glowed dully with its own hidden fire. Hagbane chuckled.

'Now we shall see what we shall see.'

She sat down opposite the tripod so that the simmering mixture was between herself and the Merestone. An empty blackness descended upon the room. The Shadow-witch started to sway gently to and fro and a low moan escaped her lips. With her eyes closed and her body swaying in rhythm she began an incantation. Louder and louder she chanted, her voice gaining in intensity. A blue flame began to hiss above the iron bowl, lighting her gnarled features with a ghostly hue. Her eyes opened, unseeing, and she grew paler and paler until she was no more than a transparent wraith. The flame hissed higher and an icy wind filled the air. Doors slammed and objects clattered. The room seemed to tilt. Formless shapes whirled about the Shadow-witch and soldiers cowered in nameless dread as she summoned every dark force she could think of to her aid.

The wind rose to a howl, the room shook and the Merestone flashed a terrible flame that shattered the tripod and its contents. Hagbane fell and lay silent.

For a long time the Shadow-witch remained unmoving on the floor, then slowly she rose to her hands and knees. A gleam came into her eye and her mouth twisted as she saw what lay before her among the ruins of the tripod. She stretched out a hand and grasped a grey rod, about a forearm's length and as thick as a broomstick, pointed at each end. The rod tingled to the touch, possessed as it was of a strange and terrible power. She clutched it greedily.

'I've done it,' she breathed. 'With this sceptre I shall rule the world. All power shall be mine. All shall despair before me!'

13

What Sorda Overheard

The next morning saw the forest alive with activity. Sober common sense returned after all the rejoicing and boasting of the previous night. It would surely not be long before the thwarted Shadow-witch sought vengeance on the forest-folk. With this thought in mind, many began to prepare for the expected assault, especially those who lived close to her castle. Indeed, quite a number decided to move house altogether, and these made their way to the vicinity of the Enchanted Glade. Others dug deep burrows and moved their meagre food supplies and scanty possessions as far underground as possible.

'Aren't you going to move house too, Trotter?' asked Peter.

'Not me,' the old badger replied with a laugh. 'I have lived here too long to leave now. And Mrs Trotter would never dream of doing so, in any case. No, we shall stay and leave our fate in Elmesh's hands.'

'All the same,' Andrew interrupted, 'you ought to have some sort of protection. I mean, I reckon you're the one she's most likely to be after.'

'Well,' smiled Trotter. 'I've got Aldred and Stiggle. They're afraid of very little, you know.'

'Yes, but . . .'

'Trotter is right.' The speaker was Oswain, who had

just entered the room. 'This moving is, I think, un-necessary, for I sense that things will not go as many of the forest-folk fear. The days of Hagbane are numbered.'

'What do you mean?' Andrew asked. 'Can't you tell us what's going to happen? We know you told Sarah some things last night but she won't say anything.' He gave a sidelong glance at Peter. 'After all, we're part of this as well, and we think we've a right to know what's going on.'

'You went to the Star Pool in the night?' Trotter asked. 'And did you find out your destiny?'

Oswain nodded, his face betraying just a flicker of emotion.

'Let us talk outside,' he said. 'It is rather close in here and since the sun is shining this morning we may as well enjoy it. You are quite right, Andrew. I do owe it to tell you more about why we are all here.'

So Trotter, the children, Aldred and Stiggle found a grassy bank and sat down to hear what Oswain had to say.

'Long ago,' he began, 'as far back in the mists of time as you can imagine, the Great Forest of Alamore was appointed by Elmesh to be a very special place in Caris Meriac. It was given a certain magic. Indeed, there are those who say that Elmesh himself walked these paths and it was his presence that enchanted the forest. As you well know, the glade retains that enchantment, since it is untouched by Hagbane's curse.'

The others nodded their agreement.

'Legend has it,' Oswain continued, 'that a small meteorite from Elrilion plunged into the forest and its impact carved out the pool. That is why it is called Elmere, the Star Pool.'

'And that is why there is a kinship between the

starlight and the water. I too have heard of the meteorite. Some say it is the origin of the Merestone,' added Trotter.

'Then it's from outer space,' cried Andrew excitedly.

'If that is what it should be called,' replied Oswain with a smile. 'One day you may find it is less "outer" than you imagine. Be that as it may, the Merestone is no ordinary jewel, for it possesses a power of its own and while it lay in the Enchanted Glade it exercised a benign influence over the whole of the Great Forest. The trees that you see around you grew tall and fair and birds of every kind and colour rested in their branches. Flowers bloomed in colours and scents that could take your breath away. But, Trotter, you know more of this for you lived at the latter end of those days.'

The badger nodded. 'Yes, they were wonderful times and I remember them well. It was during those days, before there was any trouble, that Gilmere was formed in the pool and the prophecies were delivered by the wise. Strange that.'

'And then Hagbane came?' Peter asked.

'Yes, but before that there was a day when some deep disturbance took place that seemed to affect all of creation – a disturbance that shook the very heavens themselves,' said Oswain. 'A grim foreboding fell upon people everywhere. In the Westward lands, where I come from, there was much fear and unrest. It seemed that people were always on the move but did not know where they were going. Bands of outlaws began to appear around our towns and many evil deeds were committed. It was as though we had lost control of our lives. Even the air we breathed seemed somehow threatening.

'Here, in the forest, nothing changed because of its

special enchantment. That is, until one dark night.' He hesitated. 'One day a young woman appeared from outside the forest. She came as a pilgrim to Elmere. The woman was still in her teenage years, and very beautiful, but a bitter evil had already poisoned her heart. She gazed upon the Merestone and greed demanded that she possess it.'

'Hagbane!' they breathed in unison.

Sarah regarded Oswain curiously.

'She came from your country, didn't she? And . . .'

'Yes,' he cut in before she could continue, 'and on a certain night she entered the glade again and, by some terrible magic, wrested the Merestone from the Star Pool. Clutching her glittering prize, she fled from the forest back to her own land. From that moment the Great Forest began to die. The trees shed their leaves, flowers drooped, and most of the birds perished or fled.'

'For a while we couldn't understand what was happening,' said Trotter, 'and then we discovered that the Merestone had vanished. Despair filled our hearts, for we did not know what had become of the jewel. All we heard was a rumour of a young woman visiting the glade some time before. It was not until a year later that the full and awful truth dawned upon us.'

'Was that when Hagbane returned?' asked Andrew.

'Yes,' said Oswain. 'She came with Grogs and Grims, evil creatures that she herself had had a part in producing. She erected her castle and began cruelly to dominate the forest-folk. Many who tried to oppose her died and many were taken captive, to be used in her evil experiments.'

'The wicked creature! How I hate her!' exclaimed Sarah angrily.

Oswain held up his hand.

'All was not lost, however. The Enchanted Glade closed itself off from Hagbane so that she has not been able to find it to this day. Whenever she tries, she loses her direction and comes back to where she started. That is why the glade preserves something of the former life of the forest. Only those who are unpolluted by her evil may venture there. The wise, such as Trotter and his father before him, learned to seek wisdom at Elmere and to discern the voice of Elmesh, which is why Trotter knew of your coming.'

'When my father was dying,' said Trotter, 'he passed on to me Gilmere and the prophecy that I showed to you when you first came here. Since then I have waited and listened until I knew the time of deliverance was at hand.'

'And that's when we walked in?' Peter asked.

'Yes, and then Oswain himself. The ruler who was promised from of old.'

'Where did you get your ring?' Andrew asked Oswain.

'It came from my mother. The stone that you see is part of the Merestone itself. I discovered last night when I looked into the Star Pool that she had obtained it during a desperate bid to wrest the Merestone from Hagbane.'

They gasped at this news.

'Then your mother has met Hagbane?' demanded Stiggle.

Oswain was experiencing some difficulty in speaking.

'More than that,' he replied slowly. 'I also have known Hagbane before.'

There was a stunned silence at this news. Then everyone gabbled at once.

'Who is she, Oswain?'

'How do you know her?'

'Where did you meet her?'

Before Oswain could respond to the barrage of questions, there was a sharp crack as a twig snapped in the bushes behind them.

Aldred held up his paw.

'Quiet everyone,' he urged. 'There's somebody there, I think.'

Everyone leapt to their feet, tense and alert. They stared at the unmoving shrubs. Slowly, with Stiggle leading in one direction and Aldred in the other, they encircled the bushes. Then, hearts thumping, they rushed in from both sides, only to find that there was nobody to be seen.

'Perhaps we were imagining it,' said Peter.

'I don't think so,' Aldred replied, pointing at a broken twig. 'Look, it's not safe to talk for too long outside like this. We should have been more sensible and set a guard. Spies are nothing new to the forest.'

'Yes, yes, you are quite right, Aldred,' agreed Trotter. 'We must warn everyone to be alert to the dangers. In fact, we should do that right away. I just hope not too much was overheard if anyone was listening.'

The sun passed behind a cloud and it was suddenly chilly. They shivered and nodded.

'Let's pair off and pass the message around,' suggested Stiggle.

Everyone agreed and set off to do this. Nobody, for the moment, remembered the unanswered questions; except Sarah, who thought that she knew.

* * *

Not far away, a beady-eyed Sorda watched with an oily

smile on his round face.

'Very interesting,' he said to himself. 'Very interesting indeed!'

The wizard had overheard every word of the conversation and already his mind was hard at work. Glancing about him quickly, he hurried back to Terras in their underground lair.

The other wizard was hardly in a good mood when Sorda arrived. He was till trying to put together what was left out of the mess created by the children's onslaught three days before. Not only that, but they had been on the receiving end of Hagbane's wrath for having failed to provide a sacrifice for her Grims. She had refused to listen to their explanation and warned them that if they did not improve quickly they had better leave the forest or die. The news of Hagbane's recent defeats only made them more afraid of displeasing her.

'Where on earth have you been?' snapped Terras. 'Can't you see there's work to be done? Here am I working my fingers to the bone and all you can do is wander off. I thought we were supposed to be partners. What do you think she's going to say if we don't start up again soon? Eh?'

'Far from doing nothing, I've been finding out things of great value to us,' the other replied.

'Here, give me a hand with this table, will you? Or at least what's left of it. If only I could get my hands on those children again – and those mice. What've you been finding out, anyway?'

'Stop messing about with all this and I'll tell you. By the time we've finished, my friend, we shall have our own suite of rooms in the castle itself. Now listen.'

Sorda recounted all that he had seen and heard. When he had finished, Terras' eyes gleamed. He rubbed his bony fingers together with glee.

'Heh, heh. Not only will this get us back into her good books, but it'll also destroy those children. Play this one right and we've got it made.'

'Just think, a proper spell-room and real power. Perhaps even the use of the Merestone.' Sorda's eyes glittered at the thought.

'We must go to Hagbane tonight and share our news. I'm sure she will be most interested to hear what we've found out.'

'What *I've* found out,' corrected Sorda.

* * *

That night, dark counsels took place in Hagbane's lair. The air hung heavy, thick with evil, as the trio plotted the doom of Oswain and the children.

Hagbane had received the two wizards with impatience at first and kept them standing while they spoke. But at the mention of Oswain's name her attitude changed. She sat them down, eager to know more.

'Oswain, Oswain.' A strange look passed across her eyes as she mouthed the name. 'So it's him, is it? And after all this time.'

'They spoke about prophecies,' said Sorda. 'Something about him being a ruler.'

'Pah! The prophecies are the vain hopes of fools. Don't you know that I hold the Merestone and nobody can defeat me? Nobody, do you hear?'

'Yes, your highness,' replied Terras hastily.

The truth was that Hagbane had been disturbed by the mention of Oswain's name. Although she didn't accept the prophecies, she did respect the fact that both he and the children had come as predicted. The only way to deal with her unease was to act as soon as possible, but with cunning. To achieve her ends she was quite prepared to form an alliance with the wizards. They could be dealt with at a later date.

'We must work together,' she said. 'This Oswain must be destroyed somehow and I want to do it myself. None of us is safe while he lives – do you understand?'

They nodded.

'Good. Then we will set a trap between us and lure all of them to their doom. This is what I suggest. . . .'

Three pairs of eyes gleamed in the darkness as they hatched their plot. Hagbane thought of another use to which she could put her newly forged weapon and smiled as she pictured the scene in her mind. The old score would be settled at last.

14

The Trap Is Sprung

Ever since the warning had been given, everyone in the forest walked warily, with their eyes and ears open for spies who might be lurking in the undergrowth. This was becoming more difficult for a very exciting reason – life was beginning to return to the Great Forest. Buds were swelling and leaves had started to unfold. The lone crocus had been the herald of many others and new patches of bright colour were everywhere. A new and more powerful magic was at work; but thicker foliage made camouflage that much easier, and that created problems when it came to watching out for spies.

Still more forest-folk moved closer to the Enchanted Glade. Hagbane had been ominously quiet for the past three days and tension ran high among the animals. Flashes of light had been seen coming from the castle at night and black smoke by day. Something was going on, but nobody knew what.

The company in Trotter's house could only sit and wait for the next move, since clearly there was little they could do. Oswain seemed unwilling to continue his interrupted explanations and was in a brooding mood that not even Sarah dared intrude upon. By the third day of being cooped up indoors, Peter, Sarah and Andrew were feeling thoroughly irritable. Trotter and Aldred had set out early to attend to various matters among the forest-folk, and nobody knew where Oswain had gone.

'I'm fed up with this!' exclaimed Peter. 'I'll go round the twist if we have to sit here much longer.'

'Well, what shall we do?' asked Sarah.

'I don't know, but I've got to get out of this house. Anyone want to come for a walk?'

'Yes, let's do that,' said Andrew. 'I'm fed up with being stuck here too.'

'Just mind you're careful, my dears,' said Mrs Trotter, who had overheard them. 'And don't be too long now.'

'Thank you, Mrs T. We'll watch out, don't you worry. And we've got Gilmere with us just in case.'

The weather was beautiful outside: bright, fresh and clear. Peter took a deep breath and laughed.

'It does smell good, doesn't it?' said Sarah. 'There's less of that dead smell than when we first arrived. Which way shall we go?'

'Let's follow this path,' Andrew suggested, pointing to the left.

Before long, the pleasant stroll down the meandering woodland path had them all feeling much happier. Life wasn't so bad after all and, forgetting the threat of Hagbane, they began to laugh and joke and chase one another with bits of twig.

They had been playing around like this for about twenty minutes when, all of a sudden, there was a movement in the bushes bordering the path just ahead. They each froze. The next instant, none other than Sorda the wizard stepped out in front of them. Sarah stifled a scream and Peter's hand dived into his pocket for the mirror. He was about to open it when Sorda spoke. His voice was smooth and soft.

'I wouldn't do that if I were you, young man. At least, not if you wish to see your friend Trotter alive and well again.'

'What do you mean?' Peter demanded. 'What have you done with him?'

'Not me. I haven't touched him,' Sorda sneered. 'No, Hagbane has. Or rather her Grogs. They've caught him.'

'Oh, no!' gasped Sarah. 'Not our dear Trotter. Oh, what shall we do?'

'Rescue him, of course,' snapped Peter, rather more sharply than he had intended. 'That is, if he's really been captured.' He spoke to the wizard. 'Why are you telling us this? After all, you're on Hagbane's side and you tried to kill us. It's got to be a trap!'

Sorda smiled.

'What's in it for me? Why, I'm changing sides, that's what. I want to bring Hagbane down, the same as you. And you have the power.' He indicated Gilmere.

'We don't make bargains with the likes of you,' Peter replied. 'So you can forget it. We're not interested.'

'You overlook the fact that Trotter has been captured and is not far from here. They'll be taking him to Hagbane and you know what that'll mean. I know where you can stop them.'

'I don't believe you,' Peter replied.

'Hey, listen Pete. Look, I'm not sure I believe him either, but we've got to take a chance, just in case. It would be awful if Trotter really is caught.'

'Yes, Peter, please let's check it, just to be sure,' Sarah added.

Peter hesitated before turning to the wizard again.

'You'll have to prove yourself to us. Take us to Trotter

and, if he's rescued, we'll think about what you've said. If you try anything funny I'll fry you alive. Now move!' He gestured angrily with the mirror.

Sorda flinched and, muttering to himself, stumbled down the path in front of them. He seemed to be taking Peter's threat seriously and kept casting nervous glances over his shoulder as he hurried along.

'Just keep your eyes open for a trap,' hissed Andrew. 'This path is leading us towards the old clearing, I reckon.'

'Well, we'll know soon enough if he's telling the truth – we're nearly there,' Peter muttered.

Just as he spoke, Sorda gave a cry of fright and, to their absolute astonishment, fell crashing into a hole in the path and disappeared from their sight. The children stopped dead in their tracks.

'He's fallen into a trap!' exclaimed Andrew.

'Do you think it was meant for us?' Sarah asked.

Before anyone could answer her question, all three were thrown to the ground by the weight of a huge net that was dropped on them from the trees above. After that, everything happened so quickly that there was nothing they could do to save themselves. Six Grogs leapt to the ground and swiftly bundled up the children, whose struggles only entangled them further. To his dismay, Peter realised that he had dropped the mirror in the confusion. The Grogs thrust a pole through the mesh, and, balancing it on their shoulders, carried the children at a fast pace towards the clearing ahead. They were followed by a grinning Sorda who was brushing down his clothes, having climbed out of the pit.

Sarah looked back and saw his smirk.

'That wicked wizard. It was a trap after all. I'm so sorry, Pete. It's my fault for saying we should go with him.'

'No, it's mine too,' said Andrew.

'Nobody's to blame,' Peter replied. 'Let's just hope they haven't got Trotter as well. If only I hadn't dropped Gilmere . . . '

The Grogs came to a halt and stood to attention in the clearing. Their captives watched helplessly as the waiting Hagbane, with a hand on her hip and a leer on her face, slowly swaggered towards them.

'Stupid young fools,' she mocked. 'You fell right into my trap. I've caught you good and proper this time, haven't I?'

'You're evil and horrible and nasty! I hate you!' cried Sarah. 'Let us go. Just let me get at you, you wicked old bag!'

She struggled violently in the net.

The Shadow-witch sneered. 'Your words mean nothing to me and it's too late for you to interfere with my plans now, in any case. Guards, prepare the next part of the plan. You know what to do.'

At her command, the Grogs carried their struggling load across the clearing until they came to a pole shaped like an old-fashioned hangman's post. There they dropped the children in a heap and fixed a rope to the net. One of the Grogs threw the end over the crossbar. With much puffing, the Grogs hauled on the rope until the children were suspended in the net about two metres off the ground. They struggled to readjust their limbs as best they could.

'What are they doing?' gasped Andrew.

'I don't know,' his brother replied. 'I thought for one moment that we were going to be hanged.'

'I'm frightened,' Sarah whimpered. 'I don't like this at all. If only Oswain were here. Oh, what's going to happen next?'

As if in answer to their questions, the guards returned to where they hung, carrying bundles of dried gorse from the bushes surrounding the clearing. For a moment, none of them could understand what was happening. The Grogs began to pile the gorse beneath the children.

'Is she going to drop us into it?' whispered Andrew. 'It looks ever so prickly.'

'No, I don't think so,' Peter muttered grimly, as the truth dawned on him. Sarah also realised what was happening.

'She's going to burn us alive!' she shrieked.

Her dreams came rushing back with stark vividness, and she screamed with all her might.

The three children stared, horror-struck, as Hagbane advanced on them bearing a burning branch in her hand, her face twisted into an evil leer. Slowly, a bass drum began to beat. Two Grogs put trumpets to their lips and began to blow long raucous blasts. Vainly, the children struggled as the Shadow-witch drew close.

*　*　*

In the depths of the forest everyone heard the beat of the drum and the blare of the trumpet. They stopped what they were doing and began to ask one another what was going on. Trotter and Oswain were together when it began.

'Something is happening,' said Trotter.

'Yes, we had better investigate. I suspect it is Hagbane making her move at last,' Oswain replied.

Trotter frowned. 'I wonder where the children have got to. I haven't seen them for quite some time now.'

'Nor have I, and I don't like it. Come on, Trotter, that sound is coming from the direction of the old clearing, if I'm not mistaken. Come on, hurry!' Oswain sounded grim.

They raced out of the house together and found themselves along with many other of the forest-folk rushing towards the incessant beat of the drum and the insistent blast of the trumpet. It still took some time to reach the clearing and everyone arrived puffing and panting behind the gorse bushes that marked the edge.

As they began to creep through the gorse the forest-folk quietened down. Everyone was on the watch for trouble, but they could never have been prepared for what they saw. There, hanging from the post, were the three children, and Hagbane stood before them clutching in her hand a burning torch. Dozens of Grogs stood to attention in a semicircle behind them. The monotonous sound of the instruments continued.

'They've caught the children,' gasped Trotter.

'Yes, I was afraid of that,' Oswain replied. 'So this is how it is going to happen.' He spoke almost to himself and his lean face looked taut.

'Surely she's not going to kill them,' cried the badger. 'I must try to stop her.'

He darted forward, heedless of his age or personal danger, and fearlessly approached the Shadow-witch.

'Hah! So you've arrived, have you?' she snapped,

glaring at him with venom. '*All* of you, I trust?' She emphasised the 'all'.

'Trotter, go back! Don't worry about us. Look after yourself.'

It was Sarah who shouted and the two boys joined in, entreating Trotter to return to safety.

'Take no notice of them,' snarled the Shadow-witch. 'Now listen to me. I hold all the cards, so you had better. . . .'

'No, you listen to me,' Trotter interrupted angrily. 'These children came as visitors to the forest. They mean nothing to you. Let them go. Let them go and take me instead. They can return to their own country and you will have me as your prisoner.'

Hagbane roared with laughter.

'You! Do you think I want you, you decrepit old ruin? No, you're nothing to me. You don't seem to understand, you old fool. I'm playing for higher stakes. You have one with you – a man, Oswain. It's him I want. I want him delivered bound to me. Do you understand?'

'No, no,' called the children. 'Don't do it, Trotter. Leave us.'

'If we refuse?' the badger asked lamely, already knowing what the answer would be.

'If you refuse, I shall simply set fire to this gorse and burn your friends alive! In fact, I shall count to one hundred and if the man Oswain is not delivered bound by then, they die. Now go!'

'How can I trust you not to destroy the children anyway?'

'You can't, can you? Now hurry, I haven't got all day.'

Trotter stood for a moment, trying to think of a reply.

'One, two, three . . . '

He ran back to the shelter of the gorse to speak with Oswain and the others. The Shadow-witch's voice rang out to the melancholy beat of the drum.

'Thirteen, fourteen, fifteen . . .'

'Well?' Aldred demanded when Trotter arrived. 'What does she want?'

It took Trotter just a moment to give the grim news. Aldred fumed with rage and frustration.

'She's outwitted us this time. What can we do? We lose both ways. Even a head-on charge wouldn't help now.'

'We haven't much time. We must speak with Oswain quickly,' Trotter replied. 'Where is he?'

The three children hung in dread and despair. All appeared to be lost. It was them or Oswain. If only it were a dream, thought Sarah, but she knew that this time it was happening to them for real.

'Seventy-five, seventy-six . . .' The beat went on relentlessly.

Nothing moved in the gorse. The air hung still and silent.

'Eighty-nine, ninety, ninety-one . . .'

Tension mounted to breaking point. Andrew's skin prickled.

'Ninety-six, ninety-seven, ninety-eight . . .'

Hagbane moved towards the pyre with the burning brand. Implacably, she lowered it towards the gorse.

'Ninety-nine, one hun . . .'

15

All Seems Lost

'Stop!'

The firm voice rang out across the clearing.

'It's Oswain!' cried Peter.

Hagbane looked up suspiciously and grimaced. Oswain stood tall and noble in the sunlight, in vivid contrast to the crooked old Shadow-witch. He spoke again. 'Leave the children be. I agree to your terms, Hagbane; I will deliver myself up to you in exchange for their lives. See, my hands are bound.'

He began to walk towards the Shadow-witch.

'Stay where you are,' she demanded. 'I want to be sure there's no trickery. You two!' she motioned to Terras and Sorda, who by now had joined with the Grogs. 'Go and check his bonds, and be quick about it.'

The wily wizards slunk from behind the guards and made their way with reluctance across the clearing towards Oswain, all the while looking about them for signs of a trap. There was none. Oswain stood his ground while they checked his ropes and made doubly sure of his captivity by binding another length of stout rope several times about his body and legs, pinioning his arms to his sides and making it impossible for him to walk.

'Heh, heh! Try getting out of that,' Sorda sniggered.

'It's all right,' Terras called out to Hagbane. 'He can't escape from us now.'

'Very well,' snarled the Shadow-witch, hiding her relief. 'Guards, go fetch him!'

At a signal from their captain, half of the Grogs advanced on the bound man. The children watched in silent dismay as Oswain was lifted from his feet and carried across to the Shadow-witch.

Back in the gorse bushes, where the forest-folk looked on with horror, Aldred and Stiggle fumed.

'This is ridiculous! Here we are absolutely powerless while that wicked Shadow-witch gets away with it. It makes me sick. I mean, it's stupid! She's got them all now. Why on earth did we give up Oswain as well?' Aldred demanded.

'We had no choice really, did we? He was so insistent that it was the right thing to do that we couldn't have stopped him if we'd tried. What Elmesh would wish, he said.'

'Well, I don't know about that,' said Aldred. 'I don't trust that Shadow-witch as far as I can throw her. Stiggle, get the troops ready. I want action, not negotiations. We can't just sit here and do nothing.'

Stiggle obediently ran off.

The Grogs reached Hagbane with their burden and dumped Oswain on his feet before her. For a long time there was silence as the two stared at each other. At length the Shadow-witch spoke.

'So. We meet again at last, Oswain, son of the High King of Elmar. It seems a long time. You have changed very little by the looks of you. Just a bit older.'

'What has become of you, Dorinda? You have changed so much since I first knew you. What is this evil that has ruined you?'

'I'm not ruined, Oswain. Fool! Do you think outward

appearance is all that matters? My beauty lies in my power; power that shall conquer the world. That is, when I've finished with you.' She laughed in triumph. 'Take him away!'

'Wait! You have my life in exchange for the children. That was the agreement. Release them.'

The Shadow-witch still held the flaming torch. Reluctantly, she doused it on the ground.

'Your friends can get them down. Pah!' she spat. 'I don't need them now. Not when I've got you, Oswain. No, they can go back to where they came from.'

'Let him go, you rotten old rat-bag,' Andrew shouted. 'You've no right to make him a prisoner.'

The Shadow-witch span round.

'Right? Did you question my right? I hold the Merestone, fool. I have the might – so I have the right!'

Hagbane thought this sounded rather clever so she repeated it again as she and her guards marched away from the despairing children and back to the castle, with the captive Oswain slung on their shoulders.

The moment he saw that the Shadow-witch and her crew were well clear of the children, Aldred spoke to Stiggle. 'It's now or never. Do you agree?'

Stiggle nodded. He glanced round at the animals assembled behind them. They had armed themselves with just about everything they could lay their hands on. It was time to engage the enemy.

'This is it then. *Charge!*' Aldred cried, as he led his troops at full tilt across the wide clearing. Heedless now of danger and full of pent-up fury, the animals surged towards the children and their retreating captors. They had almost reached Peter, Sarah and Andrew when

Hagbane heard the commotion behind them. She turned and her face flashed with anger.

'The cursed fools! Do they think to stop me now? I'll give 'em something to think about!'

So saying, she drew her wand from beneath the folds of her gown and pointed it with cold deliberation in the direction of the captive children. A blinding flash of fire shot from its tip, bright as the sun, and the next instant the pile of gorse beneath them burst into flame.

'Meddling fools. That'll teach them not to cross me,' she snarled.

Oswain struggled vainly in his bonds as he realised what had happened.

'Put it out, Dorinda. Please,' he begged. 'They haven't harmed you. What about our bargain?'

The Shadow-witch laughed with harsh indifference and turned on her heel. Oswain groaned. There was nothing he could do to help.

The gorse began to crackle into life as the fire took hold and smoke poured upwards, rapidly enveloping the children. Sarah screamed and the boys called hoarsely for help. Already they could feel the heat of the fire beneath them. Struggling in desperation, they began to cough and splutter and their eyes smarted in the smoke.

The forest-folk, led by Aldred, stopped short in their tracks when they saw what Hagbane had done. For an instant nobody moved, each creature paralysed by his natural fear of fire. Then Aldred leapt forward. He plunged into the burning gorse and began scattering it as far apart as possible, pushing the whole mass away from the children. The other animals reacted swiftly to their leader's example and rushed to help. Trotter swiftly

organised the remaining animals into a chain to pass
along bark containers filled with water from a nearby
stream. Vast hissing clouds of steam soon mingled with
the acrid smoke and the eager helpers were soon
coughing and spluttering.

Eventually, to everyone's relief, the flames died out
and the smoke began to clear. Stiggle found the rope
securing the children in the net and released it. One on
top of the other they tumbled out in a confusion of arms
and legs, shaken and exhausted and covered in soot.
Their eyes stood out pink and bloodshot against the
blackness of their faces as they struggled to their feet and
tottered across to the weasel.

'Oh, thank you! Thank you, Stiggle,' Peter gasped. 'I
really thought we were going to die. It was terrible.'

'It's Aldred you must thank rather than me,' he replied.
'If it wasn't for him none of us would have had the
courage to tackle this by ourselves. He just charged
straight in without any thought for his own safety.'

'Yes. You're right, Stiggle. But really all of you were
fantastic. You saved our lives.'

'By the way, where is Aldred?' Andrew asked. 'I can't
see him anywhere.'

The smoke was almost clear by now and the animals
were beginning to sort themselves out. Some stood back
to admire their handiwork with satisfied smiles on their
faces. Others, who bore singe marks here and there, were
busy checking tails and whiskers.

'Aldred? Aldred?' Peter called.

'Aldred, where are you?' cried Andrew.

There was no reply. One by one, the animals stopped
their chattering and an ominous hush fell over the crowd.

'Oh!' cried Sarah. 'Oh, no! Look!'

Everyone turned to see her pointing to the ground with a trembling finger. Folk hurried across to her. There, badly burned and quite still among the ashes, lay the brave Aldred.

Trotter bent over him. Then slowly he raised his head, his old eyes full of tears.

'I am afraid our noble captain is dead,' he said quietly. 'This is a terrible loss for every one of us.'

A stunned silence greeted the news. Then, as it sank in, a great howl of sorrow and anguish arose from the assembled forest-folk.

'He was the bravest creature I ever knew,' sobbed Sarah. 'He gave his own life to save us. Oh, I can't bear it!'

She stumbled away from the dreadful scene with tears streaming down her smoke-grimed face. For a long while, none of them could do anything but weep. But at length, Trotter spoke and his voice was grave. 'Matters are very serious for us. Our enemy has Oswain and we have lost our fighting leader. But we must not allow ourselves to go under. Stiggle, you will assume Aldred's role. Peter, Andrew, Sarah, we must talk without delay. The rest of you must return home and prepare for war. This is a dark day. Elmesh help us! Come, let's get to safety and remove Aldred from this awful place.'

Four younger stoats bore away the body of their captain upon their shoulders, walking with slow steps towards the trees and a place of burial. The stench of burnt and wet wood hung in the air and small burns began to sting in the cool wind as the sad procession wound its way into the cold shadows of the silent trees.

16

Oswain Refuses to Bow

'So, my dear Oswain, son of the High King of Elmar, and all lands Westwards; Prince Oswain, the so-called servant of Elmesh – at last I have you!'

Hagbane stood before her prisoner, gloating over her prize, her voice heavy with sarcasm. Strong chains bound Oswain to the cold stone wall of her spell-room. He made no attempt to free himself, but gazed at the Shadow-witch with a mixture of sadness and revulsion, while she rubbed her bony hands together with glee. She noticed his look.

'Can't get used to it, eh? Not like your old Dorinda, am I? What did you expect to find? Some beautiful princess? Pah! You always were stupid.'

Oswain spoke with difficulty. 'I loved you, Dorinda. You were once the fairest woman in the land and the most precious person in my life. What is this dreadful evil that has overtaken you?'

'Evil? Hah! If you call power evil, then evil it is. But I want power, Oswain. I desired it even when we were younger but neither you nor your family would grant it me. So I sought it for myself. And I found it!'

'We couldn't give you what you wanted because you had already grown evil. Pride had gripped your heart, and your rule would have brought pain and sadness upon our people if we had granted it. That is why I could

144

not marry you, even though I loved you.'

'Oh yes, you rejected me!' she said bitterly. 'I haven't forgotten the humiliation. I loathed you and your mother and I have waited a long time for the chance to destroy you and your wretched family. And now, at last, you have come within my power.'

'I did not expect it to be you I would have to confront,' Oswain replied. 'It was a deep shock when I discovered it was so in the Star Pool. I nearly turned back at that point and rejected my chosen path. Dorinda, I want you to give up this madness before the judgement of the prophecies falls upon you and you are destroyed. Make no mistake; the time for their fulfilment is at hand.'

Oswain spoke earnestly but Hagbane only laughed in his face.

'Yes, they say you've come to fulfil the old prophecies. Pah! I do not believe them. Delusion! Only fools listen to such old words – and you are a fool, Oswain – and those meddling Brown children. You think to scare me with your vague threats? It is you who should be afraid, not I!'

Oswain winced at the mention of the children.

'You broke your word, Dorinda. You killed them for no reason.'

'My word? Fool!' she screeched. 'You and your words. Words of prophecy. Words of honour. I care nothing for them. It's power that counts. Power, my dear Oswain, that I shall soon unleash upon the world. No brats or stupid animals shall stand in my way, and nor shall you. Your pleas are wasted. I will not change.'

'Then the vengeance of Elmesh will strike you, for it is from him that you have stolen the Merestone,' replied Oswain. 'What you seek to use for your own ends will turn against you and destroy you.'

'Stupid superstition! Why should I fear Elmesh?' she retorted. 'He has hardly helped you, has he? You threaten me with doom but it is you who should fear because I have the power to do anything I want to you. This is the day of *my* revenge!'

Her wild eyes gleamed yellow as she spoke. She approached him until her face was only centimetres from his.

'Do not think these are mere words, Oswain. I have created a weapon that will make all peoples serve me – or die! In fact,' she sniggered, 'I've planned to try it out on you. Then we shall see the value of your worthless prophecies.'

With a dramatic swirl of her cloak, she turned from him and crossed to a cupboard. She reached in, then faced her captive, clutching in her hand the rod that she had formed in league with the dark forces.

'With this,' she cried triumphantly, 'I shall rule the world!'

Oswain looked puzzled.

'What is it?' he asked.

'What is it? It is the power of light and darkness fused into one. It shall be terrible to behold, more powerful than even the Merestone itself, more dreadful than Grogs or Grims. With this, I shall sweep all before me.'

A madness filled the Shadow-witch's eyes as she spoke, and Oswain looked at her with horror.

'Dorinda, renounce this evil while you can,' he pleaded. 'Destroy this thing before it destroys you. I beg you.'

'Yes, you will beg, but not like this,' she answered. 'For

it is not I who will change, but you. You shall become as I am and serve me – or you shall die. That will be my revenge.'

'Never!'

'We shall see. Watch!'

Hagbane pointed the rod at the floor and muttered a spell. Oswain watched as it glowed to a bright orange. There was a brilliant flash and a vast heap of bread – loaf upon loaf – appeared before Oswain's startled gaze. She appeared pleased and muttered again. Another flash, and the bread frizzled to cinders. She turned to Oswain.

'The power to create and to destroy food. I can make plenty or I can cause famine. Who will dare challenge me with such a temptation – or with such a threat?'

She turned away and pointed the rod at the far wall. Projected there Oswain could see great multitudes of people thronging the city streets as they went about their daily business. Hagbane muttered a spell and, to his horror, fire began to consume one side of the vision. It spread rapidly, devouring everything before it. He heard the screams of terrified people, saw them fleeing madly, felt the heat of the merciless flame as it swallowed up people and property alike.

'Do you not think that it is a great power?' Hagbane demanded. 'I shall use it, make no mistake. Now watch this.'

She held the rod at arm's length, then pointed it at herself. Closing her eyes she murmured a third spell. As Oswain watched, still helplessly bound, she seemed to grow larger and larger until her menacing form towered above him. She swayed as though made of liquid smoke and then slowly evolved into a beautiful princess who gazed at him with soft, melting eyes. Oswain started as he saw once again the love of his youth standing before him. He longed to reach out and touch her and his heart was filled with the yearnings of lost love.

The vision again changed and she became a regal lady, cold, aloof, absolute in her power, looking down upon him with utter contempt. He felt the pain of rejection in his heart.

The figure doubled, trebled, multiplied until the room was full of Hagbane clones. Their faces twisted and aged until they became nightmarishly ugly, more ugly than Hagbane herself. Terror gripped him as they approached him, their long, gnarled fingers outstretched like talons to tear out his throat. The next moment, she was a sweet little girl looking up at him with appealing eyes and offering him an apple.

Then she was Hagbane herself.

Oswain's heart jumped. He realised he was trembling, and sweat covered his forehead.

'Impressive, eh? What do you think? There's nothing I can't do with this.'

Oswain remained silent.

The Shadow-witch's eyes glinted. When she spoke, her words were cold and clear. 'The demonstration is over. You, Oswain, will bow to me and serve me. If you refuse, I shall kill you.'

'I shall never bow to your evil power!' he replied, recovering his composure. 'I will no longer call you Dorinda. You are Hagbane. You have tormented and killed the innocent. May Elmesh smite you!'

The Shadow-witch's face darkened with fury and her voice rose to a wild scream.

'Fool! You dare to resist me? You shall worship me and plead with me before I am finished with you! You will call me your queen. I will have vengeance on you and your house.'

The wildness in her eyes mirrored the years of bitterness and resentment that filled her being. Slowly, she lifted the rod and pointed it with an outstretched arm towards her captive. It glowed brightly in her hand and a bolt of lightning shot from the tip. Blue fire crackled all around Oswain and his face contorted as he struggled against the dark powers that sought to break him. He twisted and turned in his bonds but not a word passed his lips. Hagbane muttered a spell and more arrows of fire pounded into Oswain's body, yet still he resisted.

'Worship me!' she screeched. 'Call me your queen, curse you!'

Her hands shook with rage and the rod glowed to white heat in her grasp. Flurries of bright sparks sprayed over Oswain and he called upon Elmesh for strength. In spite of the force of the onslaught he remained unharmed.

At length, the Shadow-witch lowered the rod.

'So, you do have some power after all, do you?' she muttered. 'Very well, we shall see about that. I shall break you, Oswain – or you shall perish.'

The Shadow-witch strode across the room and brought out her most prized possession – the Merestone itself. Carefully, she placed it on a table before him.

'Now we shall see what your power is worth,' she breathed.

She removed the cover and the stone glowed in the dark room. A humming noise filled the air and the jewel began to glow more brightly. Hagbane started to chant spells. The light increased and the hum became a roar.

'Acknowledge me or die now!' she screamed above the noise. 'Even the Merestone shall obey me now, for my rod was forged in its light.'

Oswain twisted in his bonds. His face set with concentration as Hagbane's darkness sought to overwhelm him.

'Never! Never shall I bow to you, Hagbane. I reject you. By Elmesh, I refuse you.'

'Then die! Die Oswain, son of the High King!' she cried. 'Die!'

She pointed the rod at his chest and uttered a deep and powerful spell. The rod shone like polished silver and from the inner depths of the Merestone fire began to flash. The roar became a deafening thunder and the whole room began to shake. A single beam of blue light blazed from the Merestone and struck the ring on Oswain's finger, dissolving the gold in an instant. Immediately, the sliver of the jewel it had contained flew through the air to rejoin the stone. A thunderous crash marked the uniting of the Merestone and the room streamed with light. At that very instant, Oswain's bonds fell from his hands and feet.

Hagbane was stunned and could only stare in amazement. Then, with a howl of rage, she lunged at Oswain with the white-hot rod. Light and fire spattered the walls. Lightning flashed. The ground shook beneath their feet. With a fierce twist of his body Oswain evaded her thrust and found himself locked in a desperate life-and-death struggle with the Shadow-witch. The whole room burst into flames. In this instant, a mighty earthquake shook the floor upon which they fought, rending open a wide crack to reveal a bottomless pit from the depths of which a fire burned sullen red.

Together, Oswain and Hagbane struggled on the brink of the pit while the Merestone wreaked its own terrible revenge. Grimly they fought, oblivious to the havoc around them, gasping and panting as each sought to gain the advantage over the other.

They teetered on the very edge of the chasm. Then Hagbane had him; the gleaming rod was under his throat. With a cry, she lunged upwards. In the nick of time Oswain twisted away and the Shadow-witch lost her balance. She clutched at Oswain's clothing as she struggled to regain her footing. He tried to free himself, but it was no good. She staggered back, taking him with her. There was nothing he could do as, together, they fell into the unspeakable depths of the chasm.

A long piercing scream of despair echoed up from the flaming abyss. Fire and smoke billowed out until the room was filled with flames and nothing else could be seen.

17

Into Battle

Stiggle paced restlessly up and down in Trotter's front room, his furry face furrowed with emotion. He was deeply grieved over the loss of his commander and the all too recent burial had been difficult for him to bear. Now Trotter had made him leader of the forces; Stiggle, who had always been second-in-command; Stiggle, who was good at carrying out the orders of others but who had never been one to make the decisions. And his first task was to do something about Oswain! It was a worrying business.

Peter entered the room and stood for a moment watching the weasel. He sighed in sympathy.

'I know how you're feeling, Stiggle, and . . . well, I just want you to know that I feel the same.'

Stiggle stopped pacing and turned to Peter.

'Thanks, my friend. It helps to know that someone understands.'

'I think we all do,' Peter replied. 'It must be a terrible responsibility for you.'

'What do you think we should do, Peter?'

'I'm not sure. But we can't waste time,' said Peter. 'If she's going to kill Oswain I reckon she'll do it quite quickly. We'll have to get a move on before it's too late. Then again, I suppose he may be dead already,' he finished miserably.

'If he is, or if we don't rescue him, then her power will grow even more and we'll be complete slaves. I'd sooner die than serve her evil ways, and I think most of our folk feel the same.' He looked Peter in the face. 'I don't know about you three. You're strangers here, not forest-folk. It's still a bit of a mystery to me how you ever came in the first place, but I suppose you can escape and go back to your own land. I don't know why things have gone so wrong either. I've always trusted Trotter's word and he's always been right about the prophecies but . . . well, maybe he's got it wrong this time. What are we going to do?'

'Listen, Stiggle,' Peter said. 'I know we're visitors, a bit like people from another planet and all that, but we're in this with you. Look, Aldred gave his life to save us. We would have died if it wasn't for his bravery, and I feel we owe a lot to him. I think he had the right idea in attacking, even if it didn't work out as he wanted. At least it's better than sitting around doing nothing. Then there's Oswain. We can't just go away and forget he ever existed.' A lump rose in his throat. 'No, we're willing to die too if necessary,' he concluded.

'Yeah, let's get 'em!' Andrew had slipped into the room unnoticed and now stood with his hands behind his back, looking rather pleased with himself.

'I agree, Pete. We've got to attack that evil old bag together. And guess what? I've got something that will help us quite a lot,' he added.

They waited for him to show them what it was, but he just smiled.

'Well, what is it?' demanded Peter.

Slowly, Andrew drew from behind his back a small, round, flattish object.

'Gilmere!' gasped Peter. 'Of course! How stupid! I thought the wizards had got it.'

Andrew grinned from ear to ear.

'Well, I wondered about that, but I thought I'd take a look just in case. It wasn't on the path, of course, and I was just about to give up when I saw it lying under a bush. I don't think I'd have found it if I hadn't been really looking.'

'Brilliant, Andrew. At least we've got something on our side now. Come on, Stiggle; things are looking up a bit. I think we should attack the castle and at least do as much damage as we can. Who knows, it might turn out better than we expect and old Trotter may be right about those prophecies after all.'

'Less of the old if you don't mind! Of course I'm right about the prophecies. Elmesh does not lie – even if it is all somewhat confusing.'

They jumped at the sound of Trotter's voice as he and Sarah slipped into the room through the study door. Both carried swords in their hands and were dressed in some sort of old battle uniform.

'Hey, what's all this?' asked Peter.

'Quite simple,' his sister replied. 'Trotter and I are ready to fight Hagbane. We're also quite willing to go alone if you lot want to stay at home.'

'What?'

'Yes, we've decided it's gone too far to just sit around any more. We've nothing to lose, so we're going to fight. And we're ever so glad about the mirror, Andrew.'

She smiled at her younger brother but he could see the glint of determination in her eyes. It was a sure sign that Sarah meant business.

'Oh, er, yes . . . great. Yes, we've just come to the same conclusion – we fight. Glad you want to come along,' Peter said awkwardly. He wondered why it was that old folk and girls always seemed to make their minds up quickly in a crisis.

'Right then,' cried Stiggle, feeling much happier now that a decision had been reached. 'To arms, everyone. Let's prepare the troops!'

*   *   *

So it was that a large company of forest-folk swiftly rallied to Stiggle's call. This time they were in deadly earnest, ready to fight to the death if need be. Encouraged by Trotter's example, many of the older animals joined in, proudly bearing ancient swords and clubs, and slings and staves.

Stiggle took command.

'Right, fall into ranks of six,' he ordered.

Everyone obeyed with much shuffling and good humour, particularly when Fumble managed to bring four others tumbling over with him as he tripped over his own stave.

'I give up!' groaned Grumble, who was one of those who had fallen.

Stiggle addressed his troops. 'We all know why we're here. If we don't defeat Hagbane we will be her slaves for the rest of our lives, which she may shorten, in any case. We either accept that or we fight and maybe die in the attempt. This will be a fierce battle, with no quarter given; so if anyone wants to drop out, let him do so now.'

Silence descended on the company as he waited. Nobody moved.

'All right, then let's go!' he cried. 'Death to Hagbane and all her evil! Vengeance for Aldred!'

The cry was taken up by everyone present. Stiggle gave the command, 'Forward, *march*!' and the motley army set off for the castle and whatever fate was in store for them.

The company moved at a fast pace and before long was in sight of the grim stone-walled fortress. Stiggle held up his hand and ordered a halt.

'Surprise is our best weapon, so we'll charge straight in,' he said. 'Those of you with ropes and grappling irons, use them. Those who can climb walls anyway, get up there as quickly as possible. It's important that we get the main gates open for the rest as soon as we can. Some of you, under Foxy's command, are to take the tunnel entrance through which Peter escaped. I don't think they will expect us, so there may not be many guards on duty. Even so, be ready for anything. Fight hard, and Elmesh go with you.'

He drew his sword and an eager murmur ran through the company. Nerves and sinews tightened as the thrill of battle gripped each of their hearts.

'*Charge*!' yelled Stiggle, and the army surged forwards as one. Brandishing their weapons, they flooded across the open ground in front of the castle, shouting and yelling as they ran.

Most were about halfway across the intervening space when without warning the ground trembled beneath them. It was followed immediately by a great earthen wave that heaved with such violence that many were thrown to the ground. There was dismay and confusion as they scrabbled to their feet and tottered about. Hagbane had been expecting them after all and the battle was lost before it had even started. Expecting to be swallowed up alive at any moment, many of the forest-folk dropped their weapons and awaited their fate at the hands of the Shadow-witch.

A great roar rose from within the castle walls. It was followed by an almighty crash, and then a vast sheet of billowing flame shot into the sky. Everyone stared awe-struck at the sight. Another crash, and the walls began to split and fire poured from the windows.

'What's happening?' cried Peter.

'The prophecies are coming to pass, I believe,' Trotter replied quietly as he lay beside him on the still-shaking ground. 'I think the Merestone has been made whole at last.'

The walls continued to crash down and they saw dark Grogs fleeing for their lives.

'Get them!' Stiggle commanded as he regained some control over the situation. 'Attack now, while we have the chance.'

In spite of their fear, the animals rose to the order and streaked after the fleeing guards who had for so long held them in terror. At that very moment, a terrifying screech rent the air. They stared upwards.

'It's Arca!' cried Sarah. 'Hurrah! He's come to help us.'

The mighty eagle swooped low with his fearsome talons outstretched, his shadow racing across the ground like an avenging angel. Terrified Grogs fell before him, never to rise again. Not a shred of mercy did he show to those cruel creatures who had caused such pain to so many of the forest-folk.

Sarah grabbed the mirror from Peter.

'You use your sword. I'll take this,' she cried.

Before he could argue she was gone into the thick of the battle. Weapons clashed, shouts and groans filled the air, smoke and dust choked the lungs, but on rushed Sarah towards the castle, intent on finding the Shadow-witch herself. She reached the walls and began to clamber over the rubble. A large Grog blocked her way. He raised a great sword and prepared to strike. Without hesitation, Sarah flicked open Gilmere. The light blazed forth and the Grog shrivelled to a cinder. She pressed on, and moments later she was standing in the courtyard. Buildings blazed all around her and massive beams and towers fell in noisy showers of sparks and dust. Smoke swirled everywhere as Sarah's eyes darted about in an attempt to find her bearings.

The next moment, a huge dark shadow fell across her. She turned and looked up in panic. There before her reared a gigantic Grim, like some prehistoric monster, with its fierce taloned wings outstretched, as black as night. Its eyes glared with bloodshot hatred. The long jaws snapped greedily.

Sarah fumbled with the mirror. Her hands were trembling, and she almost dropped it. The light streamed out – and missed! Her mouth fell open with horror as the loathsome creature advanced on her. She screamed and the mirror fell from her nerveless fingers, its light still blazing.

Then, just as the vile creature was about to strike, the ground shook once more and where the light of the mirror shone, a wide chasm opened. With a scream of rage the creature lost its balance and with its limbs thrashing wildly it fell into the depths. Sarah lay panting and gasping, her heart beating fit to burst. She shook with fear and her legs refused to hold her weight. She looked around for the mirror but realised, to her dismay, that it too had fallen into the abyss. She knew now that she had no weapon with which to face Hagbane.

Slowly, she rose to her feet. A firm resolve filled her heart. 'Then I will have to face her alone, in the name of Elmesh!'

A door hung from broken hinges and, heedless of the chaos about her, she stumbled resolutely towards it.

* * *

'Stiggle, Stiggle, we're winning!' Peter grinned in triumph at the weasel as they struggled towards the castle.

'Yes,' he shouted in reply. 'I reckon we've got them on the run. Oswain must be behind this somehow, you know. I wonder what he's done.'

'We'll find out soon enough now,' his comrade replied. 'Looks like the prophecies were right after all.'

It wasn't long before all the Grogs had been dealt with and the noise of battle began to quieten down. Hagbane's castle was utterly ruined. Peter, Andrew and Stiggle climbed over the broken walls and entered the wrecked courtyard.

'Phew, what a mess!' Andrew exclaimed.

'I wonder where Oswain is? And Sarah too,' said Peter.

'They must be around here somewhere. Give them a yell, will you?'

'Sarah? Oswain? Where are you?'

There was no reply to their calls. They stood in silence and waited.

'Hush! What's that?' said Stiggle.

They listened and heard the sound of sobbing.

'That's Sarah. Quick – it's coming from over there.'

Joined by Trotter, they ran across the yard and entered a room that had obviously been Hagbane's lair. There they found Sarah, begrimed with soot, sitting on the floor sobbing. Before her yawned a deep chasm from which came a dull red glow and a subterranean roar, muted by the distance. Sarah turned at the sound of their coming. She looked at them in anguish, with her tears making white streaks down her blackened cheeks.

'He's dead,' she wailed. 'I know it. And Hagbane too. They've fallen down there – into that awful pit.'

She pointed into the gaping hole.

'Oh, why did it have to end like this? He's destroyed her but he's died too. We've won, but we've lost really.'

With that she burst into tears again. The others edged towards her, peering gingerly at the great rift in the floor. Peter put his arm around his sister. Suddenly, he felt very weary. Together they gazed into the chasm but it was too deep to see anything except the red glow.

Peter spoke at last. 'Come on, Sis, it's no use staying here,' he murmured, and he helped her to her feet.

18

To the Enchanted Glade

Before anyone could do much else, the room was shaken by a deep rumble. Dust fell all about them and the half-burned timbers groaned so loudly they expected to be buried alive at any moment. As they fell about in confusion, trying to protect themselves from the falling masonry, they saw the yawning chasm begin to close up. A final crash resounded through the ruined building. More debris fell. Then, only a jagged line remained to show where the pit had been.

The rumbling and shaking ceased as suddenly as it had begun. Everyone stood coughing because of the dust, staring at the crack running across the floor.

'It's closed up,' said Andrew rather obviously.

'Yes, that's that then, I suppose,' Peter answered. 'Nothing more we can do. Though I wish I knew what that hole was all about. It seemed to go on for ever, like some kind of hell. It was horrible.'

'I don't understand it,' said Trotter. 'Except that Oswain seemed to know what he was doing when he handed himself over to Hagbane. There may be more to it yet, but I am at a loss to know what.'

At that moment, one of the roof beams began to groan and buckle.

'Come on!' cried Stiggle. 'We'd better get out of here. This room isn't safe. Anyway, we must tell the others.'

Scrambling over the rubble, they made for the door and escaped only just in time before most of the ceiling collapsed. As they came into sight a vast cheer arose from the animals assembled in the courtyard.

'Hurrah for Stiggle! Hurrah for Peter!'

'Hurrah for Andrew! For Sarah!'

'Hurrah for Trotter!'

They stood together and smiled wanly at the company gathered before them. Trotter raised a paw to indicate quiet so he could speak. He stepped forward and cleared his throat.

'My dear forest-folk,' he began. 'You have every good reason to be happy, for a mighty victory has been obtained here today. All the Grogs and Grims have been destroyed, thanks to your bravery and the assistance of Arca.'

He was interrupted by much cheering and clapping, particularly for the eagle, who was perched on a remaining part of the wall. Trotter waved for silence again.

'The best news of all is that Hagbane herself is dead.'

For a brief instant there was silence, then, as the truth sank in, the whole crowd erupted into a riot of cheering, stamping, shouting and whistling. Trotter waited patiently until things quietened down a little. Even those who knew what had become of Oswain couldn't resist smiling as they saw the joy and relief on the animals' faces. Eventually, Trotter continued.

'We are free at last to live our lives in peace and without fear of arrest or death. I cannot put into words just how much that means to us all.' His voice trembled with emotion. 'But it has not been without its cost. I see that some of you have been wounded in the fighting, but

I refer especially to our dear brave Aldred, who longed for this day, and . . . and to Oswain.'

He faltered and a murmur ran through the crowd.

'Yes, I am afraid Oswain is dead also,' he said at last. 'It appears that he died while destroying Hagbane, but I cannot say what happened exactly. The truth is, we have received some remarkable help from Elmesh. Were it not for the earthquake, things might have been very different. Part of that earthquake split open the ground in Hagbane's lair and it appears that both fell to their doom. We owe a great debt to Oswain's memory, for he willingly paid the ultimate price for our freedom . . . for the freedom of Alamore.'

A solemn silence had fallen over the audience as the full meaning began to sink in.

'Well,' said Trotter, doing his best to brighten up, 'what's done is done and I am sure it is what Elmesh wished. So, go to your homes. Tell your loved ones and your children that they are free to enjoy the forest once again. May Elmesh bless you all . . . and thank you for all you have done today.'

The crowd slowly dispersed, everybody talking among themselves about the events of the day, and soon only the little band of five remained.

'We'll pull this castle right down,' said Stiggle. 'Then we'll erect a monument to Aldred and to Oswain's memory. It'll become a favourite spot, I expect.'

'That's a good idea,' Andrew said. 'You could use the stones of the castle to build it.'

'I think I would just like to get away from this place at the moment,' said Sarah. 'Can we go?'

'Sarah's right,' said Peter. 'Come on, everyone. We look

as though we could do with a good clean up, let alone something to eat. I'm starving.'

They looked at one another's bedraggled clothes and grimy faces and then, in spite of their mixed feelings, couldn't help laughing.

'We do look a sight. I wonder what Mrs Trotter will say,' chuckled Trotter. 'Yes, let us get back and leave all our problems for the moment. Things have not been so good in years.'

Andrew spoke to Sarah as they walked slowly back. 'Maybe that's all there is to it, Sarah. We've done our part and perhaps we can go home to Mum and Dad now. I know you're upset over Oswain, but perhaps he's done his part too.'

'I don't know,' his sister replied. 'It feels so incomplete, so . . . well . . . so not right, if you know what I mean.'

'Yes, I do. But you mustn't let it get you down. Come on, race you back to the cottage.'

'Thanks. I'll try not to be too sad. But I think I'll walk back, if you don't mind.'

* * *

By the time they had eaten and cleaned themselves up, it was quite late. Nobody needed any encouragement to go to bed and before long they were all sound asleep. All, that is, except old Trotter. The badger was perplexed and sat up long into the night, staring straight ahead, lost in thought. Much later, he arose and went to his library where he began to pore over some dusty parchments.

'It doesn't make sense,' he muttered to himself over and over again. 'I wonder. I just wonder.'

It was not until the early hours of the morning that he eventually stopped and fell asleep in his armchair, with the papers sprawled across his lap.

He awoke with a jerk at around five o'clock. Outside he could hear the birds singing and the sun was already up. Swiftly and silently, he rose and left the house. The air was fresh and sweet and he couldn't help noticing that the undergrowth was looking fresher than he could ever remember, even back in the days before the troubles began. Bright green leaves cast a delicate filigree of shadows over the path as he walked. He breathed deeply in the wholesome air, then made his way resolutely towards the Enchanted Glade.

Sarah had slept heavily and without dreaming but she woke up quite suddenly not long after Trotter had left. She, too, rose quietly, noting that everyone was asleep but that somebody had left the house, leaving the door ajar. She felt sure it was Trotter and that he was on his way to the glade. With scarcely a moment's hesitation she set out to follow him.

Trotter sat on a moss-covered rock in the Enchanted Glade. The air seemed electric all around him and he felt a tingle of happiness running through his old frame. It was as though the years were falling off and he was young again. He wrinkled his snout and wondered if he actually looked younger.

He heard a rustle behind him and leapt to his feet.

'Oh, it's you, Sarah,' he said with a slight tinge of disappointment in his voice. 'I had expected someone else. But then I am not surprised that we should be here together again.'

'Hello,' she whispered. 'I just had to come. I've got this feeling that, well . . . that something very wonderful is going to happen today. I can't explain it.'

'There is no need to try, my dear. I feel exactly the same. That is why I am here. There are things I did not understand when I read the old writings last night, but when I awoke this morning I knew that I must come here and wait. Hush! What is that?'

He placed his paw on Sarah's shoulder.

'It came from over there – from Elmere itself.'

They gazed in the direction of the pool but nothing seemed to have changed. Still the pearl-like droplets dripped from the overhanging ledge with their musical plip-plop. Then Sarah cried out: 'The water! Look, it's moving!'

They gazed towards the pool and, sure enough, its surface was in a tremendous turmoil. It began to boil and bubble like a cauldron and then slowly a shape began to rise from its depths. The two watchers stood transfixed as the shape, at first formless, became the figure of a man who rose splashing from the water. An aura of light seemed to surround him and he was magnificently clothed in purple and gold, glistening with wetness. He rubbed his eyes with his hands then looked around him. The full morning sun revealed his strong tanned features and penetrating eyes. Then, fully risen, he stepped from the pool.

'It's Oswain!' cried Sarah. 'It's Oswain! He's come back!'

She raced towards him and leapt up to throw her arms around his neck.

'Oh, Oswain, it's you! It's really you!' she exclaimed.

For a moment he looked surprised and then laughed.

'Sarah! I thought you were dead! Yes, it is me. As you can see, all has come to pass as promised.'

'So I was right,' breathed the badger. 'Welcome back, Oswain, son of the High King and rightful ruler of the Great Forest of Alamore.'

He made to kneel but Oswain swiftly reached out a hand and lifted him to his feet.

'Trotter, old friend, King I am, as it is written, but I will not have one such as you bowing before me. I count you as an equal, not a servant,' he said. He gave them a warm smile. 'To be greeted by you both on my return is so delightful. And you alive, Sarah. Your brothers, too, I guess. I can't tell you how happy all this makes me. What a glorious morning! The winter is over. Springtime has come.'

He laughed again and soon all three were delirious with joy, dancing round and round with their arms thrown about each other.

'B...b...but how? W...what happened?' asked Sarah when at length they quietened down. 'How did you kill Hagbane? How did you get here? And ... and ...'

'Enough, Sarah. I shall tell you all just as soon as everyone is gathered. It won't do to spoil it now, will it? How are Peter and Andrew? Is everyone all right?'

'Yes, everyone is well except for ... but I will tell you later,' declared Trotter. 'They will all be overjoyed to see you again. Why, this is truly amazing. I can hardly wait to hear your explanations myself.'

'Well, that will not be long now, and then I will hear of your own exploits. But there is more to happen yet.

Come over here. I want you to see this.'

He led them across to the pool and plunged his hand into the water. Slowly, he drew out a glittering jewel and held it up in the light for them to see. The stone glowed with a brilliant fire that seemed to shine right through each one of them. Were it not for Oswain's presence, Sarah felt she would have been burned up by its power. She gazed in wonder.

'The Merestone,' sighed Trotter. 'You have the Merestone. After all this time.' His eyes filled with tears to see it again.

'Yes,' replied Oswain. 'And now I restore the Merestone to its rightful place, that it may never be removed again while a king reigns in Alamore.'

So saying, he placed the jewel upon the rock to the side of the pool. There was a hissing sound and the stone fixed firm. He tapped it.

'There. It is done. From this day the forest will be blessed by its presence and the latter days will be as glorious as the former.'

The three gazed reverently upon Elmesh's stone, entranced by its beauty and power.

'Can we go now?' asked Sarah. 'I'm dying to tell the others.'

'I think we may,' Oswain replied. 'Listen though. Someone's coming.'

19

Explanations

Peter's eyes opened; he blinked and looked around him. Sunlight was streaming through the leaded windows, lighting the old oak furniture with a mellow glow and making the brass ornaments sparkle. The new day smelt so fresh that he just had to get out of bed.

'Hey! Come on, everybody,' he shouted. 'Wake up!'

He gave his brother a shove.

'Wassermarra?' Andrew groaned sleepily. 'What time is it?'

'Getting up time! It's a lovely day. Come on!'

Andrew wasn't yet convinced. He snuggled into the blankets while Peter went to wake the others.

'Hey, where's Sarah and Trotter?' he called. 'They're not here.'

'Oh, they've gone out, my dear,' called Mrs Trotter from her room. 'To the Enchanted Glade, I expect, if I know them.'

'The Enchanted Glade? We'd best go after them. Don't want to miss anything. Come on, Andrew. Get a move on. We'd better hurry.'

By now, Andrew was wide awake too.

'All right, but how do we get there? I don't think I know the way.'

'Nor do I, but I reckon we'll be OK today. I just feel it.'

'Huh, you sound just like Sarah!' Andrew joked.

'I'll have breakfast waiting for you all,' Mrs Trotter called as they made for the door. 'Mind you're not too long now.' She smiled to herself as she busied herself about the kitchen.

Outside, the dew shone in the early sunshine and birds chirped in trees fresh with newly opened leaves. The sky shone blue, the air smelt clean and it felt good to be alive.

'I can't believe this,' cried Andrew. 'Yesterday, we were fighting Grogs and Grims and felt upset about Oswain, but today I don't feel tired or aching or . . . or even sad.'

'Yes, I feel the same,' his brother replied. 'Something special has happened in the night. Perhaps it's just that Hagbane is dead and the curse is lifted. Anyway, Trotter's bound to know. Come on. The path starts here. Race you to the glade.'

So off they ran and, sure enough, they did find all the right paths and it wasn't long before they arrived, puffing and panting, at the great sentinel stones that marked the entrance to the glade. Peter made it only just ahead of his brother.

'Come on, slow coach! Let's find the others.'

They stepped into the glade just as Sarah, Trotter and Oswain turned at the sound of their coming.

'Hi Sarah! Hi Tro . . . '

The boys stood speechless with their mouths hanging open in amazement. For a moment they just stared and stared. Andrew was the first to regain his voice.

'Oswain! Oswain! It is you, isn't it? B-but we thought you were dead.'

'So I was,' he replied. 'But I have returned from the darkness. Hello Andrew – and Peter. I'm so happy to see you again.'

Slowly, the two boys came forward. Actually, they both felt just a little bit awkward, though afterwards neither could explain why. There seemed to be something very special about Oswain that put them in awe of him.

'It *is* you, Oswain,' Peter whispered. 'I'm so glad. We really did think you were dead and . . . and that was all. It was so horrible.' There were tears in his eyes as he spoke.

'I have a lot to explain to you and I'll do that just as soon as – well, just as soon as we've had breakfast. To tell you the truth,' he said, 'I'm very hungry.'

He laughed and the awkwardness was broken. They all began to laugh together and it was a very jolly company indeed that romped its way back to the cottage.

Upon their arrival, they found Stiggle awaiting them. He bowed low before Oswain as soon as he realised who he was. The poor weasel couldn't cope with Sarah's garbled explanations and stood, as the boys had done, quite speechless with wonder.

'Stiggle, I am glad to see you, but where is your brave captain, Aldred?'

At this, a solemn hush fell upon them all. Trotter spoke. 'Sire, Aldred, Aldred our brave captain, has died. He gave his life to save the children when they were about to be burnt alive.'

Oswain was silent for a long time upon hearing this news.

'He was a courageous leader. We shall not let his name be forgotten. You must tell me everything and I will ensure that he is honoured throughout my kingdom,' he declared.

They were interrupted at this point by Mrs Trotter, who came bustling through the kitchen door. Trotter hurried across to his wife and briefly explained what had happened. She advanced slowly and curtsied low before Oswain.

'I've already laid an extra place for you, sir. I rather thought you might come back.'

Oswain smiled.

'Arise, great and noble lady of the forest! Trotter, you have a fine wife, and she does you proud. Come now, let us eat and do justice to her labours!'

After an enormous breakfast during which little was said to interrupt the serious business of eating, everyone strolled outside and sat in a circle on the warm grass. Eagerly, they looked to Oswain as he began his promised explanation of what had taken place.

'The early history of the Great Forest I will not repeat to you,' he began. 'You know all that is necessary, including the time when Hagbane seized the Merestone and began her evil reign. But I must take you back to a time before that; to the time of my early youth in the lands Westwards of Alamore.

'My Father, Argil, is the High King of those lands, and it has been a great kingdom for many an age. He is both wise and good and has ensured that my upbringing would fit me one day to succeed him. It is the custom in my country for the wise to speak words of good counsel to the young and, on occasion, to predict their path. Such was my case; it was told that I would not only inherit my father's kingdom but that in time I would become the legal ruler of the Great Forest of Alamore beyond the mountains. It was said that this was the will of Elmesh and that he would make known to me when this should happen. The wise also said that it would involve sacrifice and suffering to achieve this. I may say that I did not relish the idea at all.

'Then the day came – or I should say the night, for it was given to me in a fearsome dream. Elmesh spoke in a vision and I knew this was the moment. So I set out for my unknown destiny.'

'That would be when I also heard from Elmesh,' interrupted Trotter.

'Yes, and Arca too. When the time is right Elmesh speaks to many so that there need be no doubt.'

'Then we came down the tree!' exclaimed Andrew. 'But we didn't know why until Trotter explained things to us. It all sounded weird.'

'I'm sure it did,' Oswain laughed. 'It is strange enough when you know something of Elmesh's ways but even more so if you haven't even heard his name before.'

'You saw something in the Star Pool,' said Sarah. 'I think I know what, but please tell us.'

'Ah, yes, Sarah. You have a special gift indeed. Much like the wise of my own land. You must beware lest you grow too old to recognise it any more, for it is given to very few.'

Sarah's cheeks coloured and she looked thoughtful.

'Now, when I reached the forest – which I only managed after strong opposition from evil forces – I discovered that Hagbane was the foe, but I was unprepared for what would follow. I gazed into Elmere – the time that you found me, Sarah – and I saw the truth. I had known Hagbane before. She was the one I was to marry.'

All but Sarah gasped at this.

'Wow! No wonder you didn't want to talk about it,' Peter murmured.

'So she was not always like that?' queried Trotter.

'No indeed,' Oswain replied. 'She was once the fairest maid in the Westward lands. My heart was lost to her, so greatly did I love her. She was to become my wife and future queen of my kingdom.'

'What happened?' Stiggle asked.

'I spoke to you before of the great evil that seemed to fall upon the land. It was a time of disturbance and fear. Strangers came in great numbers through our country and it was one of these who poisoned my beloved's heart. Some evil seed of pride and greed possessed her and she became a changed person. Back then, I should say, she was named Dorinda. My Dorinda began to behave strangely. She grew hard and arrogant. She wanted things – gold, silver, servants. She became unbearable and my heart broke as I saw the change.'

Oswain paused for a moment.

'At length, my parents decided that she was unfit to be my bride and our engagement was broken. Dorinda was furious and swore vengeance, but then she went away and we thought that we had seen the last of her.'

'That must have been when she came to the Great Forest and stole the Merestone,' said Trotter.

'Indeed. Then she returned with it to my land, more evil than ever. She knew, of course, about the prophecies concerning my rule over the forest and I think this was her vengeance: that she should possess it for herself.

'My mother, Queen Talesanna, who is a wise woman, worked this out and confronted Dorinda. This was also shown me in the Star Pool. She attempted to wrest the Merestone from her but failed, for Dorinda had gained some power of which my mother did not know. She was defeated, but in the conflict the Merestone fell and a splinter broke off. This my mother had mounted in a ring and placed it upon my finger, sure that the day would come when the Merestone would be reunited. Little were we to know how that would come about,' he said sadly.

'So Hagbane – I mean, Dorinda – left your land?' Peter asked.

'Yes, and came to dominate this forest. Here the evil seed fully possessed her heart and she became the Hagbane you knew so well.'

'But if she was so young, how come she looked so old?' asked Andrew.

'I think evil makes people grow older more quickly than they should,' Oswain replied.

'It must have been terrible for you to know that she was your enemy,' Sarah said.

'You knew you had to meet her, which is why you let yourself be captured,' said Trotter.

'That is correct, though I never imagined that it would be in such horrifying circumstances for you children. Now you must tell me what happened after that, for I was borne away in great anguish for your safety.'

Between them they told Oswain what had followed. When they came to Aldred's sacrifice, tears filled Oswain's eyes. They spoke of the battle and of how they had discovered that Oswain must have died. All were eager to know about the events within the castle, and Oswain described Hagbane's terrible sceptre and how she had tried to conquer him with it.

'I pleaded with her to give up this madness but she had gone too far. I saw that nothing would change her and knew that I could love Dorinda no more, for she had become Hagbane for ever.

'That was when she made her mistake. She brought out the Merestone to add power to her sceptre.' He smiled grimly. 'The stone came from Elmesh and now it was time for the prophecies to be fulfilled. The stone reunited and Elmesh wreaked his vengeance on Hagbane's wickedness. The room flared and the earthquake split the floor apart. Just as you thought, Sarah, we fell together into the abyss, locked in mortal combat.'

'Then why didn't you die? I mean, why are you here?' Andrew asked. 'I don't understand that at all. I mean, it just doesn't happen, does it?'

'I cannot fully explain all that took place in the terrible depths of that pit, but we did not die as you understand death. Great forces were unleashed, light against darkness, good against evil, life against death. We ceased to be bodies as you know them but the battle continued until, with my spirit, I grasped the Merestone as mine by right and Hagbane . . . Hagbane was destroyed.'

He paused for a moment.

'I was much wearied by the struggle and wandered as a spirit through the darkness beneath the earth, only the light and hope of the Merestone guiding me. None dared touch me in that shadowy realm as slowly my strength returned and I was renewed. Then I heard the voice of Elmesh himself call me back to life. I came at last to the Star Pool where the light of Elrilion met that of the Merestone once more. Such glorious light and colour – you couldn't imagine it,' he mused. 'Anyway, in the midst of that splendour I received my body again and came up from the waters, as you saw.' He smiled towards Trotter and Sarah.

'Yes,' Trotter spoke. 'I *knew* that something must happen. The prophecies had been right all along and I could not believe they would fail now. I studied them again until sleep overtook me. When I awoke I knew the answer lay in the glade and so I came to await whatever should come to pass.'

'I think it's utterly amazing,' Peter declared. 'I mean, I've never heard of anything so . . . '

'Hoy!' Stiggle cried out and leapt to his feet. Before anyone else could move, he shot into the bushes and began crashing around.

Moments later he emerged carrying a torn piece of green cloth in his paw.

'Pah! Too late. They got away.'

'What was all that about?' asked Andrew.

'Hey, I recognise that cloth,' cried Peter.

'It's the wizard's!' Sarah gasped.

'Yes,' Stiggle replied. 'I heard a rustle in the bushes. We weasels have excellent hearing, you know. They must have been listening. Pity I wasn't a bit quicker.'

'Never mind,' Oswain said. 'They heard little to their good. I guess two wizards are, at this very moment, fleeing for their lives. They know now that the Great Forest is no place for the likes of them. Poor shadows!'

* * *

Deep in the undergrowth, two figures scuttled along as fast as their legs could carry them. The taller one slapped the other around his bald head.

'You stupid idiot! Why can't you keep quiet? They'll be after us now.'

'It's not my fault, you gawky old fool. I don't know why we had to go spying again anyway. It would have made more sense to have tried getting on their side.'

'Bah! You know nothing,' Terras replied. 'You don't think that they would want people like us, do you? Come on, let's get out of here before it's too late.'

So, still grumbling at each other, the two wizards fled the forest to seek their fortune elsewhere. But, high in the sky, a pair of fierce eagle eyes watched their going and their direction with great interest.

20

Celebrations

Sheer unbelief greeted the first news of Oswain's return. However, it took very little time for such doubts as the forest-folk had to turn into great joy. Soon they were flocking to see him, and many an evening was spent in telling the wonder of it all. Not least of the wonders was the fact that Oswain had restored the Merestone to its rightful place. Day after day, folk made their pilgrimage to gaze with reverence on the long-lost source of their happiness, and there to discover that the Enchanted Glade held even more blessings than it had in the past.

So the tale is nearly told. The Great Forest of Alamore began to prosper and flourish under Oswain's reign. Animals walked without fear; the young played with not a care in the world; food grew in abundance and everyone said it was the happiest place there ever was. All traces of Hagbane's rule were swiftly and thoroughly erased – the stones of her castle became all sorts of useful things, such as a new jetty for the river, paths, house walls and millstones. Elmere became again the place for wisdom, for healing, for young lovers to promise to be true to each other.

All this came about after some time, but there was one early event that formed a topic of conversation for many years to come. It was the great celebration.

During the days following Oswain's return there was

much planning and busyness on the part of the forest-folk. Even the children were drafted in to help Mrs Trotter with the baking. Rumour had it that this was to be the biggest feast ever! Expectations ran high.

At last the appointed day came and everybody gathered in the old clearing. How different it was from their last meeting! The sun shone upon the fresh green grass; trees proudly displayed their blossomed finery; flowers, gorgeous in colour and sweet in fragrance, filled every available spot. The air buzzed with excitement as the multitude came together. Young eyes looked with longing at the heavily laden food tables and hoped that the formalities would not take too long.

Then a long, clear trumpet call sounded. Everyone turned their attention to the dais that had been erected for the occasion. Trotter stepped forward and spoke.

'My dear forest-folk,' he began, 'I want to welcome you all to this great occasion, this time of celebration, this day of thanksgiving and of feasting.'

He paused as everyone cheered wildly. Smiling, he held up his paw for silence.

'For a number of years now I have had the privilege of being your leader. Those years were hard and sad and only by the help of Elmesh was I able to keep going. My hope lay in the promise of deliverance that was given way back in the elder days. Good folk, that deliverance has come and we are once more free. Elmesh be praised!'

More cheering rent the air.

'Now, my time as your leader is completed. My task is done. It is my joy and privilege to appoint one to succeed me as a ruler whom we can utterly trust to be wise and just.' The aged badger paused and drew himself upright before continuing. 'To you who dwell in the realm of the Great Forest of Alamore, I present Oswain, the son of the High King of the West, whom I declare your King by the will of Elmesh!'

Oswain rose and stepped forward, resplendent in his royal robes. He stood, noble features caught in the sunlight, and smiled upon the crowd. All bowed before his majesty. He spoke in a deep, clear voice.

'Rise, forest-folk, for I will not have you in fear of me. My reign must be one of love and friendship, of justice and truth, not pomp and ceremony nor threat and fear. We shall begin as we intend to continue.'

'Hear, hear,' said an old rabbit.

'Soon we shall eat and drink and celebrate together.'

More cheers, especially from the younger element in the crowd.

'But first,' he continued, 'we must express our gratitude and thanks to those who have brought us to this happy day. The foremost is old Trotter himself. For a long time he has been a faithful adviser and friend to you all. It was he who foresaw the time of Elmesh's visitation. He is the one who so fearlessly campaigned against Hagbane's evil devices. None can put into words how much he has done for the forest.' Oswain's eyes scanned the throng. 'He has stood down from leadership but I cannot fully let that be. Friends, I wish to appoint Trotter as my chief and personal adviser for the rest of his days – and may they and those of his wife be long and happy. They shall be known henceforth as Lord and Lady Trotter.'

The whole crowd rose as one and applauded this announcement, while Trotter looked a bit abashed, but nonetheless obviously pleased.

'Next,' Oswain continued, 'there are three very brave mice. Fumble, Mumble and Grumble, come forward!'

There was a rustling at the front of the crowd.

'Ouch! Silly clot! Can't you do it right even today? Get off my foot!'

'Sorry,' Fumble replied, still standing on it.

'Cumonutoo, stomonin, erwaing.'

'Oh, shush!'

The three mice made their way up the steps and bowed low before the King; except that Fumble bowed so low he fell over in a somersault and landed on his back, with his legs waving in the air. Everyone burst out laughing, much to Grumble's indignation.

'Fumble, Mumble and Grumble,' Oswain continued, once order had been restored, 'in token of your bravery I appoint you, hereby, knights of honour to accompany me wherever I go in the forest.'

The mice swelled with pride, while Trotter looked more than a little alarmed.

'Don't worry,' Oswain whispered to him. 'I shall send them to the Enchanted Glade until their, um, difficulties have been sorted out. But they are of fine heart, old friend, do not fear.'

He turned to address the crowd once more.

'We have had a mighty ally, without whom we could not have achieved this victory and we must thank him also.'

So saying, Oswain looked up and whistled long and shrill. From his lofty domain Arca, the mighty white eagle, glided to land gracefully before the King. Although the animals knew him to be a friend they nonetheless drew back before his awesome presence.

'Arca, we thank you for all you have done. I give you no reward for I know you would take none. And I ask no allegiance of you for I know you serve Elmesh alone. Yet I bid you always welcome among us and would have you know of the honour with which we hold you in our hearts.'

'It is well,' the bird croaked in reply. 'Elmesh's will has been done. May his sun warm your days and the light of Elrilion guard your nights. Farewell, Oswain. May your reign be long and peaceful.'

With a shrill screech, the eagle rose from the ground and soared upwards towards the sun until not even the keenest eyes could follow him.

'And now, good folk,' said Oswain, 'I give you the children, Peter, Sarah and Andrew Brown.'

The three children stepped forwards and climbed the steps. The crowd rose again and cheered so enthusiastically that they felt really quite embarrassed.

'These three came from far beyond the forest, even from another realm altogether. They are here at Elmesh's bidding and found themselves unwittingly caught up in our battles. Many fearsome dangers they have faced in the struggle but they have remained brave and loyal. They are an example to us all and we express our gratitude to them for all they have done. Soon they must return to their own land and time, however. I cannot bid them stay, though I gladly would. Yet I would have them remember us and know of our gratitude.'

Oswain motioned to Trotter and the latter brought forth a velvet-covered tray upon which there lay three translucent pearls of crystal. Each had a chain of gold so fine as to be almost invisible. Oswain passed one around the neck of each child in turn.

'These are solidified droplets from Elmere,' he explained. 'At least, as near as can be called solidified, for you will find that they possess a life and a power more than sight or touch can tell. Take them as a token of our thanks.'

Sarah and Andrew looked at Peter and nodded to him to say something. He blushed, coughed, cleared his throat and began: 'Er, um, well I don't know what to say really, but, er, thanks for everything. It's been a wonderful adventure but scary too and, um, well, I'm, I mean we're, glad it turned out all right in the end. And we think you really are wonderful and . . . and we're really glad this happened to us.'

He finished, still a bit flushed. The crowd applauded loudly as the three sat down.

'Well done, Pete,' Andrew whispered. 'I wouldn't have known what to say.'

'Look at these jewels,' Sarah said. 'Why, you can hardly see them they're so clear. I think they're beautiful and mine makes me feel all kind of special.'

Oswain was speaking again.

'There is one more person to mention,' he declared. 'I have left him to last because of his importance. His name is Aldred. Alas, he is no longer with us, as you all know. He gave his life to save the children as selflessly as he had lived and fought. We mourn his loss but his name shall always be honoured and remembered in our midst.'

He pointed to a large object covered with a white sheet. All had been wondering what it was but great secrecy had surrounded the project, although the sound of hammering and chiselling had been heard for many days.

Oswain motioned with his hand and four young stoats tugged at the sheet. It fell off amid wondering gasps. Revealed in shining stone was a larger-than-life statue of Aldred mounted upon a pedestal of rough-hewn rock. It really was a most magnificent sculpture and a worthy monument to the brave leader.

'From now on,' cried Oswain, 'this clearing shall be known as Aldred's Park and thus shall his name be immortalised for ever.'

A heartfelt round of applause greeted this proclamation.

'And now,' he smiled at the folk gathered before him, 'the time has come to end the formalities and to begin the feasting. Let us then make merry!'

Possibly the loudest cheer went up at that moment, especially from the younger ones, and the crowd descended as one upon the food-laden tables.

* * *

Peter, Sarah and Andrew were sitting together in the shade of a tree about two hours later, having eaten their fill of goodies and spoken to innumerable animals who wanted to thank them personally.

'Phew, I feel blown,' declared Andrew.

'Me too,' his brother agreed. 'This has certainly been some party. I wonder what time it will end.'

'I don't know,' said Sarah. 'Probably quite late, I should think. But I feel it's finished for us now, anyway. We've done what we were sent to do and I kind of feel, well, an outsider again. Do you know what I mean?'

'Yes, I agree,' nodded Peter. 'I think we should go soon. It feels a bit sad but we really must get back to our own home.'

'I suppose we can do that,' said Andrew, a little anxiously. 'I mean . . .'

'Oh, of course we can,' his sister interrupted. 'If Elmesh got us here he can get us back. I'm not worried, anyway.'

'You know, it seems bad but I've hardly thought about Mum and Dad, but I guess they'll be really worried about us. Do you think they'll be angry when they see us?' Peter said.

'No, just relieved,' Sarah replied.

'I bet they've had the police out, and tracker dogs and helicopters and the army and everything,' Andrew enthused.

'Oh, I do hope not,' said Sarah.

'Well, we'll find out soon enough now,' said Peter. 'Here come Oswain and Trotter and I have the feeling it's time to say goodbye.'

They rose to their feet as the King and the badger drew near.

21

Return to the Old Oak

The afternoon shadows were lengthening, and the air was warm and sweet with the scent of honeysuckle as the little company made its way through the forest paths. They had decided in the end that only a few should see the children off and so, after touching farewells to the animals and especially to Fumble, Mumble and Grumble, only Oswain, Trotter, Mrs Trotter and Stiggle accompanied them on this last walk through the forest.

Together, they stood for a while before the monument to Aldred. Tears flowed as they remembered how he had saved them from a horrible death, only to lose his own life. Then they paid a last visit to the Enchanted Glade. Here, the magic of Elmere restored their happiness. The Merestone radiated a soft warmth that filled the air with life and goodness, while its light now gave the falling droplets of water an even greater brilliance than before.

'What a wonderful place,' Peter exclaimed. 'I could stay here for ever!'

The others agreed before continuing on their journey to seek out a single oak tree.

* * *

'Just around here, I think,' said Trotter, breaking the

silence of the last few hundred metres.

They rounded a clump of bushes and there in front of them stood a tall English oak, the late afternoon sun shimmering through its branches. There, too, was Sarah's red scrunchie that she had left so they could find the right tree again. She ran across to retrieve it. Slowly, the rest walked to the base of the trunk, rounded it and came upon the hole that led upwards.

'Well, here we are,' said Peter with a sigh.

They stood in an awkward silence for a few moments, until Oswain spoke.

'Peter, Sarah, Andrew. We have become great friends in the brief time that we have known one another and it is not at all easy to say farewell. However, it is the will of Elmesh that you should leave and return to your own realm.'

'Oh, I wish I could stay here for ever!' Sarah exclaimed. 'I love it so much now that it's all changed. And you've become such special friends. If only we could come back whenever we pleased, but I know it's not like that.'

She bent and kissed first Mrs Trotter and then Trotter himself.

'I shall never forget you. And thank you for looking after us.'

'I don't know that I did much of that, my dear,' said Mrs Trotter. 'Seems to me that there were others who protected you when you most needed it.'

'Yes, but you made it all so warm and comfy.'

Stiggle she hugged. Oswain stooped and put his arm around her.

'Sarah, you and I have a special kind of kinship, for you possess the same gift as my mother. I want to remind you to guard it well and use it wisely to help others. Do not let the passing years take it from you.'

She looked into his eyes and nodded. Tears filled her own as he kissed her goodbye.

The two boys shook hands with the badgers and the weasel as cheerily as they could and they all wished each other well. Oswain put his arms around their shoulders.

'Boys, you have played a valiant part in this adventure, with courage far beyond your years, and you have learned many lessons about the ways of good and evil. Do not forget these as you grow up. It will not be the last time you are called upon by Elmesh, of that I am sure. Farewell, my good friends.'

Peter and Andrew said their farewells, feeling suddenly very grown up.

'Right then,' said Peter. 'Everyone ready? Let's go.'

So the three entered the warm darkness of the oak tree, waving goodbye to the four who watched their departure.

'Here are the steps,' said Andrew and began to climb.

They scrambled upwards into the darkness until a faint glow of light showed ahead of them.

'Nearly there,' puffed Peter.

Each one felt it again at the same point: a strange tingling sensation all over their bodies and the faint shimmer of light that told them they had passed through the invisible barrier. Seven steps later and they were in the short tunnel.

The next instant, they were looking down upon their uncle's orchard in the late afternoon sun.

'I wonder what day it is?' Sarah thought.

'Mum and Dad are going to be really worried,' said

Andrew. 'I wouldn't be surprised if they're cross with us – at least, until we explain what's happened.'

Just then, they heard the familiar sound of their mother's voice calling them.

'Teatime, kids. Come on in now. And don't forget to wash your hands.'

'It's Mummy,' gasped Sarah. 'Oh dear! Do you think she's been calling us every day like this? How long have we been away? Perhaps it's sent her mad. Oh, how awful! Mummy! Mummy! We're back. Up here,' she squeaked.

Below them was the smiling face and red print dress of their mother.

'So there you are,' she laughed. 'I wondered where you'd got to. Have you had a good afternoon?'

The children couldn't believe their ears. Perhaps Sarah was right and she had lost her senses because of their absence.

'Afternoon?' they repeated incredulously.

They quickly clambered down the ladder and ran into their mother's arms.

'Oh, Mummy, we're so sorry we've been away so long! It's lovely to be back safe and sound. We've had the most incredible adventure but you must have been really worried about us. Have you been very upset?'

Sarah looked up appealingly into her mother's eyes.

'Why, what are you going on about, my love?' her mother said. 'It's only six o'clock. I don't call an afternoon a long time. At least, not long enough to worry about. So what is this incredible adventure you've had?'

'But we've been away for *days*!' Peter exclaimed, looking puzzled. 'In the Great Forest of Alamore, fighting the Shadow-witch and . . . and . . . .'

He tailed off, for his mother was laughing.

'Oh, so that's it! You've been making up an adventure. What imaginations you children have!'

'But it's not,' said Andrew. 'It really happened and we were nearly killed. And there was Trotter and Oswain and Arca the eagle and . . .'

'And lots of others too, if I know you,' his mother interrupted. 'So where is this Great Forest of yours?'

'It's through that hole in the tree and down the steps inside,' Andrew explained.

'What hole? I can't see one,' she replied, squinting at the branches.

Together they looked and, sure enough, from where they stood there was no hole to be seen.

'Well . . . well, we've got medals to prove it, anyway,' said Sarah, rather upset. 'Look!'

Mum looked.

'Oh yes. So I see,' she said, shaking her head in disbelief, for there was nothing to see.

'Well, feel them then,' challenged Peter. 'Come on, Mum.'

'That's enough playing about now,' said their mother firmly. 'Hurry up, all of you. And don't forget to wash those hands! Stairs in the tree, indeed! Wait till I tell your father and Uncle Joe.'

'Parents!' declared Andrew as they walked to the house. 'Why can't they ever believe anything?'

'Kids!' mused their mother, smiling to herself.

* * *

That night, the children stood at the bedroom window, gazing up into the velvet night sky. Stars hung like jewels in the heavens and they stared in silence for a long while.

'Do you think we imagined it all?' asked Andrew.

'No, of course not,' his brother replied. 'I'm sure it happened, even if the grown-ups don't believe us.'

'What do you think, Sarah?'

'I *know* it was all real – and I don't think it's the last time we'll visit Caris Meriac, either. I can feel it somehow.'

Her brothers nodded.

Just then, one star seemed to glow more brightly than the rest. They all saw it. Then a dark shadow flitted across the sky. It was difficult to see, but the sound that followed was unmistakable. A high pitched, eerie screech pierced the gloom and sent shivers down their spines. They clutched at the jewels around their necks and almost felt them.

Unbelievably high in the night sky a great white bird winged his way westwards and, far below, three pyjama-clad children whispered his name in awe.

'Arca!'